Lily Kn

Oh, yes, she .... that no matter how much she wanted to deny the inevitable, she couldn't do it. Eve and that damned apple. The dark, sweet taste of temptation—of his mouth on hers, his hands on her body. Wherever they were headed, she was going willingly, knowing she'd be hurt in the end, because there was no way on earth she could protect herself against something so powerful, so wonderful—so compelling. For the first time in her life, she knew what it must be like to be addicted. To need—to want so desperately that nothing else in the world mattered.

And Curt Powers was the only cure.

The Passionate POWERS

*Men bound by blood, tied to the sea
and destined to be heroes.*

Dear Reader,

Our 20th anniversary pledge to you, our devoted readers, is a promise to continue delivering passionate, powerful, provocative love stories from your favorite Silhouette Desire authors for all the years to come!

As an anniversary treat, we've got a special book for you from the incomparable Annette Broadrick. *Marriage Prey* is a romance between the offspring of two couples from Annette's earliest Desire books, which Silhouette reissued along with a third early Desire novel last month as *Maximum Marriage: Men on a Mission.* Bestselling author Mary Lynn Baxter brings you November's MAN OF THE MONTH…*Her Perfect Man.* A minister and a reformed party girl fall for each other in this classic opposites-attract love story. *A Cowboy's Gift* is the latest offering by RITA Award winner Anne McAllister in her popular CODE OF THE WEST miniseries.

Another RITA winner, Caroline Cross, delivers the next installment of the exciting Desire miniseries FORTUNE'S CHILDREN: THE GROOMS with *Husband—or Enemy?* Dixie Browning's miniseries THE PASSIONATE POWERS continues with *The Virgin and the Vengeful Groom,* part of our extra-sensual BODY & SOUL promotion. And Sheri WhiteFeather has created another appealing Native American hero in *Night Wind's Woman.*

So please join us in celebrating twenty glorious years of category romance by indulging yourself with all six of these compelling love stories from Silhouette Desire!

Enjoy!

Joan Marlow Golan

Joan Marlow Golan
Senior Editor, Silhouette Desire

Please address questions and book requests to:
Silhouette Reader Service
U.S.: 3010 Walden Ave., P.O. Box 1325, Buffalo, NY 14269
Canadian: P.O. Box 609, Fort Erie, Ont. L2A 5X3

The Virgin and the Vengeful Groom

DIXIE BROWNING

Published by Silhouette Books
America's Publisher of Contemporary Romance

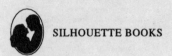

SILHOUETTE BOOKS

ISBN 0-373-76331-X

THE VIRGIN AND THE VENGEFUL GROOM

Visit Silhouette at www.eHarlequin.com

Printed in U.S.A.

DIXIE BROWNING

has been writing for Silhouette since 1980 and recently celebrated the publication of her sixty-fifth book, *Texas Millionaire*. She has also written a number of historical romances with her sister under the name Bronwyn Williams. An award-winning painter and writer, Browning lives on the Outer Banks of North Carolina. You may write to her at PO Box 1389, Buxton, NC 27920.

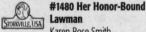

One

His bare, size-eleven feet propped on the railing, Curt let the long-neck bottle slip through his fingers to rest on the sandy porch floor. Gazing out over the Atlantic, he continued the word game a fellow patient had introduced him to in a certain Central American hospital.

Applicable words only. Even playing alone he stuck to the rules. He'd started over with the *As* once he'd settled here at Powers Point. After less than a week he was up to the *R* words. There was not a lot to do here.

Not a lot he could manage yet, at any rate.

Rest and relaxation.

Recuperation and recreation.

Nah. Scratch *recreation,* it didn't apply.

Rebuild, restore...retire? At age thirty-six?

Well, hell—how about rotting, raving, royally pissed-off?

Too much like the *B*s. Bored, bad, broken. And bitter. Yeah, that, too, but he was working on that one.

The *P*s had come easy. Powers Point. Private. Privateer?

Could his old man have been a pirate? Being the descendent of several generations of seafarers about whom he knew next to nothing, Curt had to wonder. Powers Point was a pretty valuable chunk of real estate, at least, it was now that the island had turned into a tourist haven. What about a hundred years ago? Two hundred? Why would anyone settle in a place like this unless he valued privacy and needed easy access to the sea?

Private, privacy, privateer…

It was only a word game, he told himself. He would never even have thought of it if he hadn't fallen heir to six sealed boxes a few months ago. After years of believing his father was dead, he had discovered that Matthew Curtis Powers had lived right here in Powers Point until a few years ago, when he'd entered a nursing home in Virginia, suffering from Alzheimer's Disease. Curt could have passed his own father on the street and never known it. Never even recognized him. Just thinking about it made him want to strike out at something.

He'd been on twelve-hour notice before leaving on another mission when the lawyer had finally tracked him down to inform him of his father's death. Stunned, he had accepted a deed and two keys—one for a house at a place he'd never even heard of at the time, Powers Point, and another one to a storage unit in Norfolk. He hadn't had time to absorb the knowledge—barely had time to locate a storage place and stash the stuff. Six boxes of ledgers, logbooks, diaries and old newspapers, not to mention half a dozen old novels. He'd glanced at a few of the titles and seen enough to know that he wouldn't be in any great hurry to read them.

The Virgin and the Vengeful Groom. Was that an example of his family's taste in literature?

But then, what the hell did he know about his family's taste in books or anything else? At a time when he'd been too young to know what was going on, his mother had taken him away and told him his father was dead. All those years he'd believed it, because he'd had no reason not to.

As for the boxes, he'd had little time to do more than scan the top layers, but even that had been enough to fuel his imagination. Later, lying in a series of hospital beds with nothing but time on his hands, stories his father had told him more than thirty years earlier had started coming back. Fragments. Images—things a kid might recall, never knowing if it came from a comic book or a television show or something real. Even now he wasn't certain how much was real and how much was invented out of need. Like the memory of a ship named the *Black Swan*.

He'd just about decided it was a bunch of bull when those six boxes of papers had turned up. At least some of those papers were definitely ship related, triggering a few recollections of some female relative who had grown up aboard a ship and then written a few wildly imaginative stories.

In fact, once he'd set his mind to it, he'd begun to recall quite a few tales about a family—his own, a few generations back—that had gone to sea and stayed there, men, women and children alike.

The Powers of Powers Point. He hadn't put much stock in any of the old tales as a kid. Probably more into space rangers at that age. But then, soon after that the family he'd taken for granted had disintegrated, and for the next few years he'd been too caught up in trying to understand things no kid could possibly understand to worry about his father's old stories.

They were trying to come back, though. Bits and pieces—nothing particularly outstanding, but then, memories were notoriously unreliable. Ask five men about an event that had taken place a week ago and you'd get five different stories.

So, although he hadn't put much stock in old memories, while he'd been lying flat on his back in a series of hospitals he'd had plenty of time to wonder. And, yeah, he had even wondered whether or not old Matthew might have indulged in a bit of skullduggery. Blackbeard had operated in these parts. Met his grisly end, in fact, on the next island south in the Outer Banks chain—Ocracoke.

At least it had served the purpose of occupying his mind while he waited for skin grafts to take, for broken bones to heal, for torn muscles to mend. Not to mention the time it took his body to rid itself of a variety of exotic bugs he'd caught while lying buried up to his ears in a stinking mud hole in a Central American jungle.

There wasn't a whole lot he could do yet, physically, but as soon as he was up to making the trip to Norfolk, he fully intended to retrieve his legacy and learn a little more about his past. After years of being a rolling stone, he could afford to gather a bit of moss. That didn't mean he was under any obligation to hang around, once he was back in shape.

Physically he was still a mess, but mentally he was pretty solid. Certain things were beginning to make sense to him now. Such as the way he had always felt like an alien in corn country, Oklahoma, after his mother had remarried. He'd been about eight then. His stepfather had been a decent enough guy, but they'd never been close.

Eventually Curt had joined the Navy and ended up seeing more of the world than he ever cared to see again. That was still up for grabs. His future. Meanwhile he was here in a place that bore his name, if not his imprint. Along the way he had loved and lost, as the old saying went. Loved not wisely but too well—another cliché. Alicia was a fast-fading memory he hadn't even tried to recover.

Somewhere in one of those boxes might lie the explanation for why he'd always felt drawn to salt water. Why he'd ended up choosing a career as a Navy SEAL over his stepfather's farm.

A mosquito landed on the tender flesh of a newly healed skin graft. He swore, slapped, and swore again. This recovery business was a pain in the—in *various* parts of his anatomy. Patience had never been one of his virtues. At least here he had time and privacy. The house itself was a gaunt, unpainted relic, sparsely furnished but, surprisingly enough, still solid. The outbuildings had weathered a few too many storms to be worth repairing, even if he'd had a use for them. Even if he'd planned on hanging around. As for the rest of his estate, it consisted of roughly a hundred-odd acres of blowing sand, stunted trees and muddy marsh that stunk to high heaven whenever the wind was off the sound.

Not to mention the small, private cemetery with half a dozen or so leaning tombstones. Most of the names had been sandblasted until few of them were even legible. One stood out. His father. Matthew Curtis Powers, born September 9, 1931, died, September 9, 1997. Ironic. He could think of better ways to celebrate a birthday.

Curt took a deep, cautious breath. Too deep and it hurt; too shallow and he got that suffocating feeling again. Nightmare stuff.

It's over, man. You're out of it.

Physically he was out of it. Mentally…he was getting there.

At least he had something to focus his mind on. That

helped. The nightmares came less frequently now. Once he got involved in rediscovering the father he remembered only dimly—the man who had taught him to fish when he was barely old enough to hold a fishing pole and promised that one of these days they'd buy a boat and sail to the West Indies—he'd be well on the way to full recovery.

In a week or so he would drive to Norfolk and reclaim the rest of his inheritance. While he had no intention of hanging around any longer than necessary, it didn't hurt for a guy to know something about his past—his roots.

Moving with the deceptive ease of someone afraid of jarring something loose, Curt made his way to the kitchen, squeaked open the rust-speckled refrigerator and scowled. ''Well, hell,'' he said plaintively.

No beer. Also, no bacon, no eggs—nothing but a chunk of green cheese that wasn't supposed to be that color. No more leftover pizza—he'd finished that off for breakfast. He wasn't exactly looking forward to making another supply run. Especially as he'd insisted on keeping his four-by-four instead of trading it in on something with an automatic transmission. The drive down from the hospital in Maryland had damn near killed him, but he'd stuck it out on the theory that if it hurt, it must be good for him. Once he'd opened the house up, aired it out and unloaded his few possessions, he had hauled south to the nearest village to hire a carpenter. While he was there, he'd stocked up on the necessities of life: beer, bacon and eggs and a variety of canned goods.

This time the drive wasn't too bad. The usual beach traffic, but what the devil—he was in no hurry. He pulled in at the post office to collect the accumulation of junk mail, then drove on to the nearest supermarket. It was late August. The place was mobbed. As a rule he did his shopping before eight in the morning or after ten at night. If there was one thing that galled the hell out of him—and actually, there were several—it was having strangers stare at him as if he were some kind of freak. So he had a few scars—so what?

So he walked kind of funny. So what?

Kids were the worst. They'd stare at him, half scared, half fascinated. As if he were a carnival display or something instead of a guy who'd happened to get in the way of a few pounds of miscellaneous scrap metal. "You ain't seen nothing, kid," he was tempted to growl. "Wait till I take off my pants."

But of course, he never did. His own mama, bless her frivolous, lying soul, had taught him a few manners before he'd left the nest.

Bracing himself not to use the shopping cart as a walker, he started with the *A*s and tossed in a couple of apples. Next, he grabbed a few cans of beans, some corned beef, bread and beer. Enough of the *B*s. He moved through the alphabet to cookies, candy, cheese and coffee, then located the eggs. His unwritten list was another of the mental exercises designed to keep his brain from atrophying. By the time he'd done pickles and preserves, he'd had enough. Skipping ahead to the *V*s, he opted for a copy of today's *Virginian Pilot* instead of vegetables. He had canned beans and pickles, after all.

Three days after she'd brought them home, Lily still hadn't got around to finding putting-places for the contents of a single box. She was too caught up in exploring her treasure trove. Organizing could wait. Imagine, a diary written more than a hundred years ago. For all she knew, she was the first person to read it since the woman named Bess had made the last entry.

"Okay, Bessie, where did we leave off?" she murmured. "We were hiding from that jerk who had locked up your crew, right?" Propping her feet on one of the boxes, she opened the diary she'd been reading. The stuff was gold, pure gold. Diaries, travel journals—and she hadn't even started on the novels yet. Six boxes full of who-knew-what wonderful material. It was better than winning the lottery.

The handwriting was better formed than her own, but it was still hard to read. Now and then Lily had to look up a word in the dictionary. Even so, it was amazing how a woman of the twenty-first century could slip into the skin of a woman from another era. Bess Powers had grown up in an unorthodox way and gone on to do her own thing.

So had Lily. They had both overcome amazing odds to make something of themselves—Bess in an age when women were supposed to be seen and not heard, to wear corsets and bustles and high-top shoes.

She'd even smoked cigars. Lily didn't smoke. She didn't drink. She didn't even take aspirin for headaches or cramps; however, she occasionally allowed herself to over-indulge in junk food.

"You'd have loved subs, Bessie. With peppers and onions and provolone and oil and vinegar—we'd have royally pigged out."

Bess had eaten raw fish aboard ship and something called salt horse, which might be horse, or it might be kangaroo, for all Lily knew. Neither animal sounded particularly appetizing. She had picked and eaten fruits that Lily couldn't even pronounce, much less visualize. Lily wanted to believe she would have done it, too, in Bess's place, because the more she read, the more convinced she was that she and Bess Powers were two of a kind, separated by a century, give or take a few years.

It was almost as if fate had guided her that day. She had

gone to the storage unit to leave a box of books—author's copies of her first three paperbacks, plus a few foreign copies. Doris, her housekeeper, threatened to burn the things the next time she tripped over them, but there was simply no more room on her crowded bookshelves. That was when she'd noticed the auction. A few people were bidding on the contents of three units on which the rental payments had fallen too far behind. Standard procedure, she'd been told when she'd asked what was going on. "But that's awful," she'd said at the time, even as she edged closer to get a look at what was on the block.

The boxes had been opened. Nothing but old books and some old newspapers—the others only glanced and turned their attention back to the two chairs, three bicycles and a suitcase of winter clothing.

For reasons that hadn't made sense at the time, and hardly did even now, Lily had felt defensive on behalf of the papers. Poor things, no one had wanted them. Lily knew what it was like to be shunned. Sensible or not, she'd gone all defensive and put in a bid on the lot. At least she could give the things a decent burial. Burn them or something. Maybe even try to locate the owner.

Feeling self-righteous, she had taken a second look and discovered among the ancient newspapers what appeared to be travel journals or logbooks, a few old novels, the covers all mildewed, and several diaries, the locks no longer effective as the leather straps had more or less disintegrated. That was when she'd first felt it—that all-but-imperceptible quiver of excitement that always came when she hit on the seed of a solid plot. Sometimes it was the people, sometimes the conflict—this time it was a woman named Bess, who had written diaries.

Diaries that Lily was increasingly certain she'd been meant to find all these years later, because she and Bess were kindred spirits. Oh, yes they were, and if that sounded spooky, so be it. She didn't have to admit to anything, all she'd had to do was pay for the stuff, drag it to her car, squeeze it in and get it home and up to her third-floor apartment.

Which she had ultimately done, her appetite whetted by the promise of mystery, tragedy, possibly even romance....

The boxes had been heavy, her car was small. Enter the second coincidence, or as Lily preferred to think of it, the second omen. She was of two minds when it came to publicity. Personally, she hated it. As Lily O'Malley, bestselling novelist, she had learned to tolerate it, although even the best publicity was not without dangers. Occasionally a fan grew somewhat...obsessive.

She'd been struggling to load the boxes on a dolly to get them to her car when she'd sensed someone behind her. Braced instinctively for trouble, she heard the man say, "Hey, aren't you Lily O'Malley? My wife reads everything you write. I thought I recognized you from your picture inside the back cover."

She eyed him warily. He was wearing an Atlanta Braves cap. The press pass clipped to his pocket looked legitimate, but with what had been happening to her this past week—the phone calls and the awful things she'd found in her underwear drawer—she didn't dare take chances. If this guy turned out to be her stalker, she would just as soon confront him here in a public place, where one loud scream would bring help.

On the other hand, if he really was a reporter, she would rather not be discovered wearing her oldest grungies. Hardly the image her publisher liked her to present.

Never show fear, she reminded herself. Cardinal rule. "And you are?" she demanded in her most imperious tone.

"Bill DeSalvo, *Virginian Pilot*. Whatcha got here, books?"

He looked harmless, but then, so had Ted Bundy. "Nothing at all valuable—mostly old papers. Actually, I'm really not sure yet."

"Bought yourself a pig in a poke, huh?"

"You have a way with words," she said dryly. After hearing his voice, she was pretty sure he was not the one. In fact, he was a fellow writer. So she ventured a smile, but a quick one. Not a particularly warm one.

"Let me give you a hand with that stuff." By the time he'd helped her lift the last box and squeeze it into her open sports car, she had gleaned quite a bit of information. She knew, for instance, that his wife read a chapter over her breakfast every morning and three chapters before she fell asleep each night, which didn't say a whole lot for their marriage.

DeSalvo learned that the boxes contained old logbooks, a few moldy novels and the journals of a woman who seemed to have spent some time at sea. He also learned that Lily's latest title, *Blood Will Tell*, was due to hit the stands within days and that she would be appearing at a local bookstore. And yes, of course she'd be delighted to sign a book for his wife.

Asked where she got her ideas, she nodded to the boxes. "Who knows? I might have just bought six boxes of ideas."

The young man jotted down a few notes. "You mean you do this kind of thing all the time, looking for inspiration?"

By then Lily had learned that DeSalvo was brand-new at his job, and that running into a celebrity was a big break. Flattered in spite of herself, she told him about the time she'd paid eighty-five dollars for the diary of a nineteenth-century prostitute only to find that it was a combination account book and recipe book. "All I learned was that bay leaves keep weevils out of cornmeal and that the diarist earned a grand total of two dollars a night, six nights a week and paid someone named Leandra ten dollars a month."

"For what, bed, board and clean sheets?"

"Probably."

It was then that she'd noticed the photographer he'd waved over. "D'you mind?" the young journalist asked, and she brushed back her hair and tried to look as glamorous as possible, wearing the ancient white shirt and baggy slacks she'd put on to deal with the accumulation of books Doris kept threatening to burn.

And now here she was, piling up still more stuff to trip over. Pack rats didn't need housekeepers, they needed warehouses and bulldozers.

"Hope you find something in there worth all the trouble," the young reporter had said when she'd climbed behind the wheel.

"Or at any rate something more intriguing than budgets and household hints," she returned, laughing. This time the flash caught her with her mouth open and her hair blowing across her face. Oh, well. Any publicity was supposed to be better than none at all. "There's bound to be something here. A bit of mystery, a bit of romance—who knows what I'll find?"

She waved and backed out of the parking slot, muttering under her breath, "Just don't you dare refer to my books as bodice rippers."

"The hell you say!" Curt's feet hit the deck with a jarring force that caused him to wince, swear and catch his breath. He had read and reread the piece in the *Pilot*. It was the picture of a laughing woman that had first caught his attention. Something about the way her windblown hair swirled around a face that was more intriguing than pretty—the way her shirt was lovingly plastered over small, high breasts. It was only when he'd read through the two short columns the second time that something struck a nerve. Storage unit? Six boxes? Papers, ledgers, journals and a few musty old novels?

"When asked where she got her ideas, the novelist replied that ideas were everywhere. 'Glimpses of strangers. Snatches of overheard conversation. A few lines in a newspaper. Ideas are never the problem, what's hard to find is the time to do them all justice.'"

Ideas, hell, the woman was a common thief! Unless he was very much mistaken, those boxes piled in the back seat of her toy car were his own personal property!

Not that he was into material possessions, other than his dive gear and his wheels. Naturally, those were top of the line. If creature comforts had been a priority, he would never have holed up in a place like Powers Point. He was into solitude. Solitude, singlehood and simplified living.

But dammit, what was his was his! Just because he happened to miss a couple of rent payments on a dinky little storage locker, that didn't give those jerks the right to auction his stuff off to the highest bidder. It wasn't as if he'd had nothing better to do than keep up with such trivial details. He'd gone all the way to hell and back serving the interests of his country. Fighting terrorists, arms dealers and drug dealers, who were more and more often turning out to be one and the same, hardly fell into the category of a nine-to-five job.

He didn't care *what* was in those boxes, his father had wanted him to have them, and he was damned well going to have them, and Miss Lily O'Malley could get her ideas from the city landfill as far as he was concerned.

It took three days to locate the woman. The drive to Norfolk took longer than it should because he'd had to get out every fifty miles or so to work the kinks out of his carcass. First thing he did was find a motel, check in and stand under a hot shower until his eyelids began to droop. After that he dried off and ordered in a pizza. He fell asleep with a half-eaten pizza before him and an open phone book, roused just enough to fall into bed and slept for ten hours.

Most of the next day was spent in tracking down a woman who obviously didn't want to be found. The phone company was no help at all. Gave him a hard time, in fact. When he'd pressed he'd been told that the woman had been having trouble with crank calls and that he could talk to the police if he insisted. He'd declined the offer.

Next he tried the storage company, but the birdbrain in the office spouted the company line. Skip three months and you're dead meat. Company policy.

He refrained from telling her what she could do with her company policy and tackled the newspaper office, with no better luck. City directory? Sorry. He was an officer in the United States Navy? Big deal. They had naval officers running out their ears here in the Norfolk area.

Curt still had a few sources of information not available to the general public, but as national security was not at issue, he wasn't about to pull rank over a bunch of old papers and the works of some nineteenth-century hack writer.

It was at a public library that he finally got his first lead. Lily O'Malley would be appearing at a local bookstore to sign copies of her newest book between the hours of twelve and two the next afternoon.

Bingo.

Thanks to a friendly, informative librarian, he also learned that the lady had earned herself a nice collection of awards and was on the way to building a reputation writing something called romantic suspense. What he couldn't figure out was why a successful contemporary writer would fork over even a few bucks for the scribblings of an obscure nineteenth-century spinster who, according to what little family legend he could recall, had made a career of distorting the truth.

At the bookstore he spent ten minutes checking out the site, pretending an interest in astrology while he watched a table being set up, complete with lace cover, flowers, posters and a stack of books a foot high and five feet long. If they were expecting to sell that many copies, he'd better move the hell out of the way or get crushed in the stampede.

Nobody stared at the shiny new skin on the side of his neck, or if they did, they were discreet about it. He'd worn khakis and a black T-shirt, something to blend in with the Saturday-afternoon crowd. His hair had grown shaggy since he'd left the hospital. The gray seemed more pronounced, but all in all, there was nothing about him that should spook a lady writer.

After rethinking his initial plan to confront and demand, he opted for diplomacy. A brief, polite explanation, followed by an offer to repay whatever she'd laid out, after which he would collect his property and leave.

"I hate this, I really do," Lily told herself as she shoved her lucky roller ball pen in her purse, dropped her purse in her tote and let herself out the door. No matter how many signings she did, she always got butterflies. What if nobody came? What if she had to sit there for two hours, trying to appear friendly and approachable when she felt like hiding in the rest room? What if no one showed up? What if they did, but not one single book sold?

It could happen. Once, in the early days of her career, before all the mergers had done away with the small distributors, she had spent two hellish hours in a huge discount store at 6:00 p.m. on a Friday, before towering stacks of her third paperback novel. Four sales reps, all young, all built like football players, had lined up behind her, arms crossed over their chests. Not a single person approached her table. When she'd taken a rest room break halfway through the ordeal, she'd overheard one woman wondering who she was and another one saying, "I don't know, but she must be important, she's got all those bodyguards with her."

After all the those slimy phone calls she'd been getting from some creep who got his jollies by talking dirty to women, not to mention the fact that someone—the same creep, she was sure of it—had actually been inside her apartment, she almost wished she did have a few bodyguards. Not that she couldn't handle herself in a pinch, but all the same… *Deep breath, Lily. You can do this. You've done it a dozen times before. This is only one teeny little bookstore, not a five-city tour.*

It was still hard to believe—sometimes, even now, she had to pinch herself—but people took her at face value. The bookstore manager had baked cookies and brought a lace tablecloth from her own home. Lily was so touched she felt like weeping. Nerves did that to her, and her own had been stretched to the breaking point. Her best friend, who was also her agent, had urged her to get out of town until the police could do their job. Instead, she had done as they suggested and changed her unlisted number, changed the lock on her door and had a chain installed.

That had hurt. One of the things she loved most about her apartment was that it was in such a safe neighborhood, half the time when residents visited someone else in the building, they left their doors unlocked. And while she had never quite gone that far, she'd never felt threatened. Until now.

At least here in broad daylight, in a busy mall bookstore, she should be safe.

There were already several people glancing this way, looking as if they might be coming over. The woman with two children—the teenage girls with the pierced eyebrows. The man in the black T-shirt...

Mercy. She would willingly go back to "clinch covers" if he would agree to pose. What was there about dangerous-looking men? she wondered. Men with dark, slashing eyebrows, shaggy, sun-streaked hair, unsmiling mouths and lean, hawkish features?

Hawkish features? Lily, my girl, you sound like a writer.

Then there was the way he moved, as if he had ball bearing joints. She could imagine a dancer moving that way, or a hunter silently gliding through the forest. Odds were this man was no dancer. There was no shotgun in evidence, which meant he probably wasn't on safari, either. He could be one of those foreign correspondents who put on a battle jacket to stand before a camera and read a script, or he could be—

Oh, God, he was—he was coming over here.

What if he was the one?

Ohmigod, ohmigod, ohmigod.

He's not going to hurt you here, not out in public!

Where was the security guard? Every mall had security

guards, because stuff happened. There were creeps everywhere.

Uncapping her pen, she gripped it in her right fist and lowered her hand to her lap. Smile, Lily, smile! Don't let him know you're afraid, bluff! You can do it, you're an old hand at bluff and run. Besides, even if he turned out to be her crank caller, the policewoman had told her that nine times out of ten, crank callers were harmless. Pathetic losers who couldn't interact with women except anonymously.

The last thing this man looked was harmless.

He was staring at her. Now he was moving in her direction. Years of soft living had taken its toll, because she was suddenly having trouble breathing. Surely someone was looking this way—someone would notice if he started anything? The store manager—

"Miss O'Malley? I believe you have something that belongs to me," he said in a voice that could best be described as chocolate-covered gravel.

It didn't sound like the voice she'd heard on the phone, but voices could be disguised.

Her mouth was so dry she couldn't have spit if her pants were on fire, but she forced herself to look him in the eye. Coolly, graciously she said, "I beg your pardon?"

Two

I beg your pardon?

Lily was tough. She had grown up tough. In the neighborhoods where she'd spent her formative years, toughness was a prerequisite to survival. Over the intervening years she had moved countless times, to different cities, different states. She had learned how to dress, how to speak, which fork to use for oysters, which to save for cake. The one thing she had never quite managed to do was lose the urge to slip away rather than confront trouble head-on.

And this man, whether or not he was actually her crank caller, was trouble.

"I said, you have something that belongs to me," he repeated, never breaking eye contact. Her fingers tightened on her Montblanc pen, the one she had treated herself to after her first book went to number two on the bestseller list and stayed there for three weeks. As a weapon it was slightly better than car keys. As a reminder of who she was and how much she'd accomplished, how far she had come from the skinny kid who had scrounged for food from restaurant garbage, worn clothes snagged from backyard clotheslines because she didn't dare risk getting caught shoplifting, it served well enough.

She opened her mouth to beg his pardon again, snapped it shut and looked around for mall security—for anyone bigger and tougher than the man towering over her.

"If you'd like to buy a book, I'll be—"

"I'll pay you whatever you laid out for them." Unblinking. She'd heard of unblinking eyes—probably used the phrase herself a time or two. This was the first time she had actually been confronted by a pair of deep-set, intensely blue, unblinking eyes.

How the dickens could a man make her feel threatened and dithery at the same time? She'd been threatened by experts. The crank caller who insisted on telling her in detail what he'd like to do to her made her want to kick him where it would do the most damage. The creep who had actually invaded her home, leaving disgusting things in her underwear drawer!

But dithery? The last time she could remember feeling dithery was when she'd been offered her first three-book contract after her first book had gone back to press five times. Getting a grip on herself, she said in her best *Masterpiece Theater* voice, "I'm sorry, but you've obviously mistaken me for someone else."

He glanced at the nameplate: Lily O'Malley, Bestselling Author. His unblinking eyes shifted to the newspaper clipping mounted on a poster along with one of her publicity stills. He said, "I don't think so. Look, you'll be finished here at two? Why don't I come back later, and we can settle things then?"

Totally confused, Lily watched him turn and walk away

in that odd, gliding way he had of moving. In a woman it would have been called graceful. He could have balanced a book on his head. In a man it was something else altogether. Subtle? Scary? How would she describe it as a writer?

She knew very well how she would describe it as a woman. In a word, sexy. He might not be the weirdo she had first taken him for, but any dealings with a man like that could definitely be classified as a walk on the wild side, and what woman hadn't been tempted at some time in her life to walk on the wild side?

Not Lily, though. Thank you very much. She'd been there, done that.

Turning her attention to the woman who was examining one of her books, she eased into her famous-author mode. "What do you think of the cover?"

"Well, it's real pretty, but I'd rather see who the story's about," the woman replied with a faint frown.

They discussed covers. They discussed her last two novels. By that time a line was forming, and Lily tucked the dangerous-looking man into a compartment of her mind and shut the door. It was another of her talents—compartmentalizing—that had stood her in good stead over the years. Some doors had not been unlocked in years.

A few never would be.

So that was Lily O'Malley, Curt mused as he sought out the food court and ordered a pastrami on rye with horseradish. She didn't add up. Classy didn't quite say it all. Neither did sexy. Yet she was both of those and more. *Intriguing* was a word that came to mind. He reminded himself that he wasn't here to be intrigued, he was here to get back what she had stolen from him, legally or not, and get the hell back to the island, where he could take his own sweet time going through it.

The more he thought about it, the more important it became, now that he was the Powers in residence at Powers Point, even if only on a temporary basis. As far as he knew, he was the last of the lot, and while the concept of family had never meant much to him personally, the least he could do for those responsible for his existence was to hang on to what they'd left behind. For a professional rolling stone, it was a pretty heavy responsibility, but what the hell—he'd shouldered heavier loads. He could do that much before he moved on again.

Lily signed a respectable number of books. She'd done better, but she had also done a lot worse. She accepted a number of compliments—graciously, she hoped—and one or two criticisms: there wasn't enough sex; there was too much sex; did the guy in her last book, or did he not, ever pay for that apple? She hadn't said.

She answered each critic seriously and wished the stint would end. Fourteen minutes to go. After that, a few more minutes spent thanking the staff, and she'd be free to leave.

Idly she wondered about the dark-eyed stranger with the sexy way of walking. He'd claimed she had something of his—which was absurd, of course. She'd heard just about every pickup line in the books. Some people said the most outrageous things in an effort to grab her attention.

A few went even further.

Ten minutes and counting. "I'm so glad you liked it. It was one of my favorites. Shall I sign it for you? Adella...that's a lovely name."

Seven minutes to go. No one in sight. Lily reached for her purse, capped her pen and felt around with her feet for her shoes.

And then, there he was. Those same slashing eyebrows, several shades darker than his streaky tan hair. She hadn't imagined the intensity of those eyes, nor that odd, sexy way he had of walking, as though his legs moved independently from his torso.

"Are you ready?" he asked.

"I beg your—"

"You've already begged it. If you're about finished here, why don't we go someplace where we can talk?"

"Look, Mr...."

"Powers," he supplied. "The name ring any bells?"

Powers. The voice might not have rung any bells, but the name surely did. *What have we got here, Bess?*

"If this has something to do with those old papers I bought at the auction—"

"I figured it might come back to you."

"There's nothing to discuss. It was a legitimate business deal. The things were up for sale—I bought them, ergo, I'm the—"

"Ergo?"

"What is your problem?" she demanded, rising to her full height, which was almost five feet eight inches, now that she had her shoes on again.

The store manager appeared, a questioning look on her round face. The man who claimed his name was Powers towered over both of them. "Just trying to decide on where to go for a late lunch," he explained with hard-edged geniality.

Ignoring eyes that sliced through her like a welder's torch, Lily forced a smile. "If you'll excuse me, I'd like to wash the ink from my hands."

There wasn't a single smudge on her hands. She'd visited the washroom less than an hour ago, but if there was one lesson she had learned early in life, it was how to avoid trouble. She might look like a sheltered hothouse flower—it was an image she had deliberately cultivated, in keeping with her name—but she was far more like the kudzu vine that thrived in the most barren places, surviving droughts, floods, sweltering heat and withering frost. If there was one thing Lily prided herself on, it was being tough. If there was one thing she was good at, it was avoiding direct confrontation.

Emerging a few minutes later, she saw Powers talking to the manager. He was obviously the type who enjoyed impressing women, and Mrs. Saunders was visibly impressed.

Lily was not. At least not enough to impair her sense of self-preservation. Head down, she crammed her small purse in the large canvas tote she was never without and slipped behind the reference section, then out into the mall to merge with the crowd.

Early in life she'd been forced to become a chameleon, able to blend in with her surroundings, to disappear—to do whatever it took to avoid trouble or to keep from being sent back to whatever authorities she had managed to elude. During those years between the ages of eleven and fifteen, after she'd run away from a drug-addicted mother and her mother's series of abusive men, she had managed, against overwhelming odds, to keep herself safe in an extremely hostile environment. Desperation was the mother of invention, she reminded herself as she unlocked her car, slung her tote inside and sat behind the wheel, unmindful of the dark-clad figure who watched from the shadow of an enormous evergreen outside the main entrance.

Lily had been a mean, homely kid. She'd been told that too many times not to believe it. As a woman she was mean and plain. The miracle was that she had never quite lost the ability to dream. In the end it was that very ability to escape into a world of her own invention that had led to where she was today.

She had stolen her first book before she could even read, shaping stories in her head to match the pictures. Once she discovered public libraries, she'd spent hours browsing, puzzling out words, afraid to ask for help, afraid of being chased out into the cold. Not until years later had she realized that the kind librarians probably knew why she was there, if not who she was. No matter how many hours she spent in that magic kingdom, they had left her in peace. Often they even "found" an extra sandwich that needed to be disposed of.

It was there that Lily had discovered kindness. Discovered a world—a whole universe—she had never dreamed existed. Once the doors closed behind her and she emerged into the real world again, she had carried that dream in her heart like a talisman.

Her writing career had been a fluke from the start. She'd been working at a car wash by day and cleaning offices at night when she had impulsively bought herself a package of cheap ballpoint pens and a spiral notebook. Writing had quickly become addictive—embellishing the harsh reality she knew with the fragile budding dreams she had somehow managed to keep safe inside her all through the years.

Next she'd bought a used, manual, portable typewriter from Goodwill. A year later she had stoked up her courage, marched into a publisher's office where she'd cornered a startled editor, shoved a manuscript at her and growled, "Here, read this!"

It wasn't supposed to happen that way, especially not when the editor she'd approached worked for a company that published technical books. By all rights she should have been kicked out on her skinny behind. She'd been terrified, which always came out as belligerence. But evidently something in her attitude had captured the woman's sympathy. She had glanced at the first page, then the second and then reached for the phone.

Hot target! Take it out! The words rang in his ears.

But that was then, Curt reminded himself, and this was now. The lady might be hot—his internal sensors had registered that right away—but he had no intention of taking her out, in either sense of the word.

He waited until just before dark. Timing was vital. Go in too soon and she'd still be on guard. Wait too long and the evidence could disappear.

How the devil had she managed to handle those heavy boxes, anyway? A couple of them probably weighed more than she did.

Yeah, timing was vital. Planning, too, only he didn't know how to plan this particular mission any more than he already had. Get in, get the job done, get out. SOP. Standard Operating Procedure.

Downstairs in a lobby that smelled of pine-oil cleanser, he checked the registry and found one L. H. O'Malley on the third floor. It was an old building. He would have figured O'Malley for something more modern. Something with a swimming pool and wall-to-wall parties. He eyed the elevator and reluctantly opted for the stairs. Climbing wouldn't be comfortable, but he still had an aversion to being confined in an enclosed space.

Upstairs in the apartment that had until recently been her safe haven, Lily went through her routine. Lock the door, fasten the chain, then cross her fingers and play back the messages on her machine, praying any calls would be from her agent or editor.

"Hello, Lily, this is me, your best fan. What are you wearing? Have you taken off that pretty thing you were wearing in the store today? I was there, Lily. I stood so close I could smell your perfume. I almost touched you once, but you were busy signing books. Did you like my gift, Lily? I straightened your panties—they were all jumbled up. I bet you'd like it if I—''

She switched the machine off, swore in her old Lily style, and then took a deep breath. ''Forget it, you creep, you're not yanking my chain again, not tonight.''

Deep breath, flex shoulders, do one of those yoga thingees...'atta gal, Lil!

Carefully she removed her pearls, hung up her suit and blouse and peeled off her panty hose, tossing them at the hamper. After a few extravagant movements that bore little resemblance to any recognized exercise regimen, she headed for the kitchen to make herself a mug of cocoa. Even in the middle of summer hot chocolate was her favorite comfort food. There'd been a time when any food at all had been a comfort food, but now she could afford to pick and choose, and like millions of other women she chose chocolate.

And she needed it now. Oh, damn, oh, damn, oh, damn! Just when things were going so well—number two on the bestseller list, with a new contract in the works—and this creep had to go and ruin everything! She'd been told that crank calls were a part of being a high-profile woman living alone. She'd set herself up by being successful.

Or rather the PR firm her publisher used had set her up.

Thirty minutes. She would reward herself with half an hour of pleasure, because after all, she was between books. She didn't have to start on her next one quite yet. And the signing had gone well today—she had sold more than half the stock and signed the rest. The manager had mentioned another session when *Blood* came out in paperback.

''I've earned this, and no slimeball with a damned telephone is going to take it away from me," she muttered. Sliding open the drawer of the side table, she grabbed a package of cheese crackers. Opening one of the diaries, she munched and read and sipped, thinking, genuine pearls and fancy pens are okay, but this—this is *real* luxury. What more could any woman ask?

For twenty-five of those minutes she followed Bess down something called the Chesapeake and Albemarle Canal, trying to imagine what it had been like to be a woman alone with three men in a small open boat. Not only had Bess been up against heat and mosquitoes, she'd constantly had to fight against the kind of male chauvinism that had prevailed in those days. What was a parasol, anyway? Something to wear? Something to spray on you to keep from being eaten up by mosquitoes?

Another word to look up and add to her growing vocabulary.

She read a few more paragraphs and murmured, "Way to go, girl," as she reached for another treat from her chair-side cache. At five before the hour, she reluctantly laid her book aside, dusted the crumbs from her fingers and untangled her feet from the ratty old velour bathrobe. Her agent, Davonda Chambers, had called that morning to say that the contract was ready for review.

"You know I won't understand a word of all that legal mumbo jumbo, Davie. If you say sign it, I'll sign."

"Oh, you are my worst nightmare, girl. Look, it's your career we're talking about here, not mine. You're going to read every word, and then I'm going to Mirandize you."

"Okay, okay," Lily had laughed. "Bring on your whereases and heretofores."

Davonda had made a growling noise, but she'd laughed, too. She knew better than anyone about the great gaping holes in Lily's education. Schooling had not been a priority in Lily's youth. Thank God reading had.

She wished now she'd put it off until tomorrow. Even without the stress of the past week, with that nutcase ruining her life, playing lady for any length of time was exhausting. Here in the home she had made for herself, she could relax, think about her work in progress—or think about nothing at all. If she wanted to sleep all day and write all night, it was nobody's business but her own. She did the tours and signings because her publisher had more or less mandated it—another new word—and because she knew for a fact that it had a direct bearing on her sales. The one today, for instance, would probably gain her a few new readers, and that would multiply exponentially, in the words of her publicist. Lily had come home and looked up *exponentially* to see if it was going to be good or bad. Given a choice, she'd much prefer to put on her oldest sweats, stock up on junk food and get on with the task of disappearing into the nice, safe world of fiction. She could write her way into all sorts of trouble, knowing that she could write her way out again. It was...exponential.

But even without the overeager fans and the few cranks, there'd been changes in her nice, comfortable lifestyle once she started showing up regularly near the top of the bestseller lists. Not all of them were to her advantage. Like luck, success was extremely fragile. One flop—one disappointing sellthrough, and it could all go up in smoke. So she juggled her career, dealt with her fans, most of whom were wonderfully supportive, and tried to ignore the few who weren't. She listened with half an ear to the experts, afraid to trust in today or to look too far into tomorrow because she couldn't quite forget yesterday.

The doorbell caught her halfway to her room to change

into something presentable. Other than the police, the locksmith and the pizza delivery man, the only people who knew where she lived were her agent and her housekeeper.

"You're—" Early, she'd been going to say, already reaching for the chain. Her first impulse was to slam the door. Her second was to scream bloody murder. She was still debating when the phone rang.

"The cops are already on the way," she lied, shoving hard at the door that was blocked open by a big, water-stained deck shoe.

Behind her, the machine picked up, and she heard the familiar whispery voice. "Lily...guess what I'm doing right now. I'm in bed, and I'm not wearing nothing, and I've got your picture right—"

"Oh—damn!"

Confusion, impotent anger, frustration—embarrassment—it was too much. She closed her eyes and leaned against the door, never mind that his foot was still in the crack.

"You want to tell me what's going on?" Curt pushed against the security chain, half-tempted to extricate his foot, walk away and forget he'd ever heard of Lily O'Malley. He didn't need any more complications at this point in his life.

Trouble was, the officer-and-gentleman stuff had been drilled into him at an impressionable age. Regardless of the fact that she was either an outright thief or a conscienceless opportunist, she obviously needed help. "Open the door, O'Malley." He made an attempt to sound reassuring.

She was not reassured. Glared at him, in fact. "Look, I don't have time to play games," he growled. His back was acting up again, thanks to yesterday's long drive and a night of trying to sleep on a bed that was too short, too hard, in a room where the window was sealed shut. His left leg still hadn't forgiven him for those three flights of stairs.

"Or maybe you enjoy dirty phone calls? Some people even pay for the privilege of crawling through that particular gutter."

She closed her eyes. Her face, already pale without the war paint, grew a shade whiter.

"Okay, if that's the way you want to play it, I'll just state my business, you can hand over my property, and I'll get out of your hair."

"Property?"

He did a quick countdown, trying to hang onto his temper. "I believe I mentioned before that you've got something that belongs to me?" He wouldn't have been surprised to find the lady in the process of sneaking out with all six boxes, after the way she had tried to elude him at the mall. He had let her get away, just to see what she was up to, but the game was over.

"Look, just hand over the boxes and we'll call it even. I won't prosecute and you can get back to your—"

"You won't what?"

"Uh…prosecute?" Indignation wasn't precisely the reaction he'd expected.

"Look, for your information, I don't have one damned thing that belongs to you, and what's more, I'm tired of jerks like you who won't give up!"

"*You're* tired? Well, that's just tough, lady!"

Jerks like him? By the time he had tailed her here, nearly losing her twice in rush hour traffic, found a parking space a block and a half away, jogged the distance on concrete sidewalks and then climbed three flights of stairs, what little patience he might have been able to scrape up had eroded down to bedrock.

"If you want your friend to quit calling, sic the cops on him. The advice is free. Now you can hand over my personal property. I won't even press charges."

"Charges! What charges? You're crazy, you know that? I'm going to call 911 right now and report—"

"Fine. Then you can explain how you came to be in possession of six boxes of my personal, private property!"

Gray eyes. Clear as rainwater. You'd think a woman with eyes like that couldn't hide a damned thing, but she was hiding something, all right. Guilt, obviously, because if she'd been innocent, she wouldn't have run away. "I'm waiting. Want to make the call or shall I make it for you? I've got a cell phone in my truck."

She was leaning against the door now, one hand gripping the edge so hard the tips of her fingers were white. She wasn't anywhere near as cool as she would like him to believe, not by a long shot.

He shoved his foot another inch through the crack and hoped to hell she didn't throw her weight against the door. His metatarsals were about the only bones that hadn't been busted at one time or another in his colorful career. He would kind of like to keep it that way. "You going to call the cops?"

"The cops," she repeated numbly.

"Right, O'Malley. The men in blue. So I can reclaim my boxes and you can get your boyfriend off your back. That is, if you want him off your back?"

Heavy sigh. Her fingers slid down the edge of the door. They both knew she was fighting a losing battle—evidently fighting it on two fronts. Hell, even the U.S. armed forces had trouble doing that in these days of military cutbacks. "Miss O'Malley? You want to talk about this?"

Somewhat to his surprise, a few protective instincts kicked in. It was part of the code every SEAL team operated under, only this was no team operation. If there were rules to cover a situation like this, he'd never heard of them. With his back on the verge of spasms, his left leg giving him fits and his gut complaining about the pastrami and horseradish he'd had earlier, he had to reach deep for patience. "Look, there's obviously something going on here. You need to call 911. I can wait out here, or I can wait inside. Either way, I'm not leaving."

Small gasp. Could've been a sob, but he didn't think so. And then the chain fell and she opened the door. Roughly 110 pounds, swathed in a shapeless velvet tent, hair spilling over her shoulders like a dark waterfall, not a speck of color in her face except for those wide gray eyes...and she was mad as hell. Ready to knock his head off.

Ignoring an inappropriate and totally unexpected sexual response, he held up both hands. "Unarmed, see?"

She backed down half an inch but still had that pit-bull look on her face. He couldn't blame her. Evidently there was more going on here than six boxes of stuff he owned and she was trying to claim. "You want to make that call now or shall we get our personal business done first?"

"Personal business." She was stalling, trying to come up with a good story, so he pushed a little harder.

"We can do this the easy way, or we can fight it out in court. Your choice."

"You're still upset about those *papers?* I've got this fruitcake who won't let me alone—someone breaks into my apartment, meddles in my *underwear drawer,* and you're worried about some *papers?*"

Oh, boy. "You want to run that by me again? Your underwear?"

"It probably wasn't you, because you were right here at the door when he called, but...but—oh, dammit, I am so *tired* of this...this harassment!"

"It's happened before?" He was inside her door now, automatically sizing the place up. A few nice pieces—way too much clutter. Potted plants, books, papers—bottom line, it looked like a cross between one of those house-and-garden spreads and a city dump.

"It happens almost every day. Not the…the flower and the awful underwear, but the calls."

"The, uh, awful underwear?"

"Some creep left a rose and a pair of really disgusting panties in my underwear drawer day before yesterday, and then he had the nerve to call me and brag about it. I just want it to stop!"

"Have you reported it?"

"Well, of course I've reported it, what do you take me for, an idiot?"

He didn't think she really wanted him to answer the question, and so he didn't. "What did they advise?"

She wrinkled her nose in disgust. "Change my phone number, change my lock—go on an extended vacation until the creep loses interest."

"And?" Curt prompted. He needed to get on with his own business, but no officer who called himself a gentleman would walk away, leaving a lady in this much distress. Not that he was much of a gentleman—in name only, maybe.

And not that she was that much of a lady.

"Oh, I did it all—the works. The caller missed one day, and then he started in again. I hope he fries in hell. I hope he catches an awful disease and rots from the toes up. Slowly!"

"Remind me never to tick you off," he said dryly. "Uh, about the other. My boxes?"

She took a deep breath and crossed her arms over her small but definitely feminine chest. "Look, whether you like it or not, I bought those boxes. They're mine, along with whatever happens to be inside them, end of argument.''

"End of defense argument," he corrected smoothly. "Now it's my turn."

"I'm expecting my lawyer at any moment. If you have anything further to say, you may take it up with her."

"All prepared, huh? Lawyer already on the hook. I'd say that's a pretty good indication of guilt."

"Just what is your problem, Mr. Powers? Hearing or understanding?"

"My problem? I think I stated it pretty clearly, but for the record those papers you took from my storage unit are my property. I lost them through no fault of my own."

"The sale was perfectly legitimate. I have a receipt to prove it."

He could have told her what she could do with her receipt, but he had better manners. Marginally. Instead, he gave her a smile that would have done credit to a barracuda and deliberately allowed his gaze to move over her, from the crown of her head to her bare toes.

She was tall?

He was taller.

She was tough?

He was tougher.

Two sets of arms crossed over two chests. Full battle stations.

Lily did her best to stare him down, but her best wasn't working. There was a crude name for this kind of contest. Little boys—and even big ones—were equipped for it. Women weren't. Even so, if it weren't for this other thing that had her nerves so ragged that all she wanted to do was run and bury her head under a blanket, she could have taken him, easy. At least she could have run.

Only she had nowhere left to run. It was all she could do when she thought about that creepy voice not to cry, and she had never been a crier, not even in the bad old days. So she took another deep breath and offered him the smile she had perfected in front of her bathroom mirror. Lily the Diplomat. Lily the Gracious Lady. "Tell you what, Mr. Powers, why don't you leave your card and I promise I'll let you have anything I don't need, once I've had time to go through it. Is that acceptable?"

Smile still in place, she looked him directly in the eye. She knew better than to look a strange dog in the eyes, but as a last resort it occasionally worked on bullies. Having come up through a tough school, she had seen her share of both, including her mother's so-called boyfriends, one of whom had locked her in the basement and tried to starve her into letting him teach her "a new game."

"My card," he repeated, sounding as if he might actually be considering it.

Way to go, girl! She lifted her shoulders in an elegant shrug, something else she'd practiced in front of a mirror. "Or you can jot down your address and I'll mail them to you."

"Or we can look through them now and I'll save you the bother of shipping them. My truck's parked just down the street."

Behind her the phone rang again. She froze. "You going to get it?" he asked.

"The machine will pick up." It was probably only Davonda, telling her she wouldn't be able to make it tonight. The creep almost never called twice in the same evening.

The answering machine cut in. They both listened as the familiar voice began to whisper his filthy insinuations. Lily bit her lip to keep from screaming. She grabbed her cocoa mug and would have hurled it at the phone, but Curt moved swiftly past her and picked up the receiver. "You want to run that by me again, sir? I'm not sure our technician caught that last phrase."

Waiting until he heard the dial tone, he softly replaced the receiver. "How long has this been going on?"

"A-about a week. Maybe eight days?" She was doing her best to hide the tremor in her voice, but her best wasn't good enough. "The police are working on it, but evidently crank calls aren't a high priority. They couldn't even do anything about...about the stuff in my drawer. When I told them I would never in this world buy anything so disgusting for myself, they only looked at each other—you know, the way men can do. Besides, there was no evidence of a break-in." She lifted a pair of stricken eyes. "Which means somebody—some horrible pervert—has a key to my home."

Something inside him shifted, coming dangerously close to sympathy. Being threatened by an unseen, unsuspected enemy was nothing new for someone in his line of work, but for a woman—a civilian—

He had to remind himself that he had a legitimate beef with her. He would do well to leave her and her problems to the Norfolk PD and get out before she undermined his mission.

"Lily—Miss O'Malley—I happened to be out of the country when the rent on my storage locker came due."

As he'd hoped, the diversion pulled her back from the edge. "Tough. That's your problem, not mine. Besides, I was told they gave you notice."

"Unfortunately, I was delayed. Still haven't caught up on all my mail. It's possible I might have missed a payment, but that doesn't mean—"

"Try three payments."

"Three? That many, huh. Well, the fact remains, the

stuff's morally mine. I can understand why you might think otherwise, but now that we understand each other, I don't see why we can't settle things now, and then I'll just get out of your hair and leave you in peace.'' He figured she was bluffing about the lawyer, but if he had to, he could deal with it. One way or another, he needed to settle this business and get out of town. Back to where he could breathe, where he could do his own thing—or not. Where he could damn well sleep in his own bed until he was ready to move on.

Gnawing on her lower lip, she appeared to be considering his offer. *Leave your lip alone, dammit. If it needs chewing, I'll chew it for you!*

She smelled of wildflowers. Once on a training mission he'd crawled on his belly through a whole field of the things. He would never forget the scent. ''Well?'' he prompted when she seemed reluctant to respond.

''I'm still thinking.''

''There's nothing to think about. The stuff belongs to me. I'll pay you whatever you paid—double it, for your trouble—but one way or another, I'm taking those boxes with me.''

''Who was Bess Powers to you?''

''What?''

''I've been reading her diaries. She was a writer, too. Actually that's only one of the things we have in common. She wrote novels and travel pieces for a newspaper under the name E. M. Powers, but I know it was Bess, because she covers some of the same material in her diaries. Did you know that back in those days women weren't allowed to do much of anything? But she did it, anyway. Did you know she was raised at sea aboard her father's ship? Well, of course you did—after all, she had to be kin to you if your name really is Powers.''

If his name really was Powers? "What the devil—you think I'm lying about my identity?"

"Not necessarily. I don't have any proof, though, do I? That you're who you say you are."

Easy, man—no matter how tempting that elegant neck of her looks, you probably can't get away with strangling her. "I believe she might have been my, uh, great-great-aunt or something." He'd been too young when he'd heard his father talking about his seafaring ancestors to remember much about them. His father had been merchant marine, off and on. After they'd split up, his mother claimed his father had walked out on them, but they'd been the ones to leave—she'd told him at the time they were going on an adventure. When he'd cried to go home again—a hotel hadn't seemed like a great adventure once the novelty wore off—she'd said they weren't going back, she didn't want to hear any more about it, and that she knew best. After that she'd refused to allow his name to be mentioned. Hurt, angry and bewildered, Curt had simply wanted his father back. Wanted his old life back. Not until years later had snatches of the old stories he'd heard as a child come back, usually triggered by some experience in his own life. By then he wasn't sure how much was true and how much was a combination of wishful thinking and imperfect memory.

Now, figuring it would be to his advantage to claim kinship with anyone mentioned in any of the papers, he said, "Sure she was kin to me. They all were—all the people in those papers. That's why I want them back, they're the only record I have."

"What about the *Black Swan?*"

His eyes narrowed. "What do you know about the *Swan?*"

"I've been reading. Mostly Bess's things, but some of

the other stuff, too. It's not easy reading. I mean, sure, your ancestors were literate and all that, but I've got to tell you, except for Bess's stuff, it's pretty heavy going.''

"Why waste your time and effort? I'll reimburse you and take the boxes off your hands and you can get on with your life.'' He waited. "Best offer. Take it or leave it.''

She shifted her weight to the other foot, cupped her elbow in her hand, her chin on her fist. "Well, you see, the thing is, Bess and I have this thing in common—''

He nearly blew then. Came too damned close. Luckily his training cut in just in time. Discipline and control would get him what he wanted. A direct attack would only get messy. Messy, he didn't need. Neither did she, because she had enough of a mess on her hands without a custody fight.

Trouble was, when it came to women, his negotiating skills were sparse to nonexistent. Getting physical was out. Calling her a thief might not be the best way to go, either. Diversionary tactics might work again. "You say this stalker's been bugging you for over a week now?''

"A while. Eight days.'' They were both playing their cards close to their respective chests. He glanced at her chest, then quickly looked away. No point in muddying the waters any more than they already were. The truth was, they both had a right to whatever was in those boxes, and while he figured his was the stronger claim, he couldn't deny she might have the law on her side.

The law. "And the cops can't do anything, right? Because there was no evidence of a break-in?''

"I told you that,'' she snapped.

"Did you consider taking their advice and leaving town until things cool off? Obviously, you're what the creep's after. If you're not here…''

"Fine. I get out of town, and then you come in and take what you want, is that how it goes?"

"Well, sure," he said, hurting, feeling mean, wondering how he'd gotten himself mired in the mess in the first place over a bunch of papers he really wasn't all that interested in. He flexed his fingers. "When I pick a lock, I don't leave any evidence. So go ahead—report what's missing, and then we'll see who has the best claim."

She'd started to pace, her shoulders all hunched, arms wrapped around her body as if she were freezing. In August, no less. "I wouldn't know where to go. And anyway, what about my work?"

"Take a paper and pencil."

"Oh, that's great advice. Thank you very much."

"Glad to be of service. So now, how about you show me where you've stashed the boxes, and I'll get 'em out of your way." He glanced around at the comfortable, but definitely cluttered room.

"The boxes don't take up all that much room, they're not in the way."

They were dancing around, each one trying to gain the high ground. "Oh, and don't forget to include that book over there on the chair. Looks like one of dear old Aunt Bessie's diaries."

She closed her eyes, looking as if she were praying...or trying to figure out where to kick him to do the most damage. Strong, fragile, gutsy and vulnerable. Hell of a combination. He'd been trained to come in hard, fast, and silent—to get the job done and get out. He hadn't been trained to offer comfort and protection—at least, not the kind he wanted to offer this woman.

"Give it up, O'Malley, you know you're outmatched," he said softly.

For a long time she didn't speak. Didn't look at him,

but stared at the musty old book on the seat of the uphol-
stered rocking chair. If she was deliberately trying to throw
him off the scent, she'd find out that he was an old hand
at creating a feint as a diversion while the real action was
taking place somewhere else.

Turns out, she was even better at it than he was. "We
could compromise."

"Compromise? Now, look—"

"Just hear me out. I'm willing to do this only because
I'm under a certain amount of pressure. I've got a contract
in the works, which means I'll have to be here to—"

"What compromise?"

"I'll share. You can come here for, say, two hours every
morning and we'll sort through everything, and then you
can take what I don't need and—"

"Need? What the devil is this garbage about *need?*"

She looked ready to take a swing at him. Instead, she
said patiently, "I'm really into Bess's story. It's…it's sort
of like we're bonded. I mean, think of it this way—she
was a writer, I'm a writer. She was an independent woman,
I'm an independent woman. I think she needs her story
told, and I'm the logical one to tell it, only I need all those
papers until I can decide which ones are about Bess and
which aren't. Technically, they're all mine, but you can
have those that aren't directly related to Bess."

Curt raked both hands through his hair. He'd been standing ever since she'd let him inside. Another five minutes
and he'd be ready for traction. "All right, let's talk about
both our problems. You say you're willing to share—I can
live with that. You say we can spend a couple of hours
every day here in your apartment, where there's not
enough room to swing a rat by the tail—where some cretin
keeps bugging you on the phone. Great working atmo-
sphere, huh?"

"Well, what do you suggest? That we haul all six boxes to a neutral place and camp out there until we sort everything out?"

"Bess ever mention a place called Powers Point?"

"So what if she did? What does it have to do with anything?"

"I'll tell you what it has to do, lady—as much as I hate to say this, it's probably the best answer to both our problems."

Three

Closing the door a few minutes later, Lily leaned against the cool white surface and wondered if she had completely lost her mind. What happened to the survival instinct that had kept her relatively safe growing up in the worst neighborhoods of Boston, Baltimore and Detroit? Too many years of soft living? With everything else that was going on in her life, *he* had to happen to her.

The man was an enigma. Another of her new words. And that was only for starters. Not only did he affect her mind, he affected her body, and she could have sworn she was immune to that sort of thing. Actually, immunization hadn't been all that hard to maintain, since she hardly ever encountered a man capable of overcoming years of conditioning. Not that she didn't look. And think. And wonder.

But that was as far as it ever went. As far as she allowed it to go. For years she had managed to keep herself safe.

No big deal. Early exposure to the seamiest side of life had built up so many layers of defense it was a wonder she could function, much less write about the kind of romance that existed only between the covers of a book.

Thanks to her own stubborn refusal to give up, plus a few years of counseling, she'd been functioning just fine until recently. She still went out of her way to avoid men she found too attractive, which wasn't all that difficult. According to her few close women friends, her standards were unrealistically high. They blamed it on her profession.

"Hey, no man can live up to Lily's standards, right, girlfriend?"

So far, no man had. If she'd needed a test, it was just possible she'd found one. Curt Powers was not only attractive, he was intriguing, mysterious and sexy enough to arouse instincts she could have sworn were stone-cold dead.

But he had something she wanted, and she had something he wanted, and until they could settle on who got what, they were going to have to deal. "Bess, I'm not going to let you down, I promise." Just because she would rather avoid trouble whenever possible, that didn't mean she was a coward. If something was worth fighting for, she could more than hold her own.

It had to be fate that had led her to that particular place at that particular time. Fate that had prompted her to bid on half a dozen cartons that could have been filled with useless junk from someone's attic. Instead of useless junk, she had found a kindred spirit, a woman who had something to say and needed a spokesman. Spokeswoman.

"I'm here for you, Bess. One way or another, we'll get your story told," she said aloud, feeling not at all self-conscious, because she often talked to herself. Tried out dialogue. Argued. And if occasionally her characters argued back, it was nobody's business but her own.

One thing, though—if she was going to hang on to Bess's material long enough to get her story told, that meant she was going to have to do business with Bess's great-great-whatever. *Business* business, not monkey business. No more letting herself be distracted by the shape of his mouth when he shaped his words. No more letting her imagination off the leash, which she was inclined to do, usually at the worst possible times.

So she'd noticed him. What woman didn't watch men? That's what sunglasses had been invented for. Of course, in her case it was purely research, nothing personal. He might look like a storybook hero—he might even smell like one, all sun-washed male, with a hint of some citrusy aftershave. But he was even more persistent than she was, and that she didn't need at the moment. For all she knew, he might even be married, with a wife and a houseful of children.

Lily had come a long way, but she'd never claimed to be perfect. When it came to weaknesses, she could list her own right down the line. She was still a tad too defensive. She was inclined to be a pack rat. She wasn't neat, but then, that was why she had Doris. She couldn't cook, although she was a whiz at sandwiches. She couldn't spell, but her computer could. Her grasp of grammar, let alone all the other little refinements in a writer's bag of tricks—well, she was still working on all that. So far she'd been able to fake it.

Her editor said she had "voice," which meant she didn't have to speak perfect English. Colloquial was just fine. She even knew how to spell colloquial, because she'd come home and looked up the word. Actually, she was inclined to soak up the voice of whatever writer she was currently reading, and right now she found herself thinking in Bess Powers's voice.

Or at least the way she imagined nineteenth-century English would be spoken by a woman who'd been raised with a bunch of rough sailors.

The phone rang. She tensed, then sighed when Davonda's rich contralto flowed into the room. "Sorry I got held up, I'll be by in about ten minutes with the contract. Can't stay, though. Got a date with one prime hunk. Dinner and who knows."

That was Davonda. Twice married, twice divorced, ever hopeful.

Lily pulled her hair back and tied it with a scarf, splashed cold water on her cheeks and picked up three days' worth of newspapers she'd never got around to reading. To avoid thinking about the wretched mess her life had become, she focused on the man she had fought to a draw over six boxes of old papers.

Why did he limp? He'd covered it earlier today with that sexy glide, but tonight he hadn't bothered. How had he been burned? Not from any careless household accident, she was willing to bet. Once when she was about ten, her mother, stoned, as usual, had shoved her against an oil heater. The whole place could've gone up in flames, but Lily had grabbed the heater before any oil spilled and set it upright. In the process she'd burned big blisters on both hands and one wrist. She could still remember the incredible pain. She'd tended the blisters herself, using soap and water and cooking oil, and wrapping them with a Grateful Dead T-shirt. Amazingly, they had healed without infections. Even the scars had finally disappeared, although she was still a little light in the fingerprint department.

She was willing to bet Curt's burns hadn't come from

any oil heater. A few years ago she might have asked. She had better manners now, having worked at it for years by reading every book on etiquette she could find and watching the way other women behaved under different circumstances. Not that she didn't slip up occasionally, but she was good at covering any gaffes. One interviewer had even called her charmingly unselfconscious.

If he only knew. She had practically wet her pants when he'd used a word she didn't know in a question she didn't know the answer to, and so she'd done what any well-bred lady would do. She had sneezed delicately into her lace-edged handkerchief, accepted his automatic blessing, and changed the subject.

So, Lily, she asked herself now—how would a well-bred woman behave toward a man who pushed every button she had, plus a few she'd never known she possessed?

"If she had half a brain in her skull, she would run like hell," she muttered, and gathered up two days' worth of clothing to toss into the hamper.

There was packing to do, and then she'd better let Doris know she would be out of town a few days and ask her to water the plants. Lily had a brown thumb, but she had hopes that pretty soon her flowering whatchamacallits and her hanging thingamabobs would sprout new leaves or buds or whatever. She had always wanted houseplants. All the pictures in the house magazines she used to pore over in the library were full of plants. Big muscular things with shiny leaves the size of hubcaps. She'd made up her mind before she was twelve that if she ever had a home of her own, she would have herself a jungleful of lush growing things, even if she had to postpone buying furniture.

So far her apartment didn't look much like the pictures in the magazines, but then, she'd only been at it for little more than a year. Plants took time, even with Doris to keep her from drowning or starving them.

Glaring at the phone, she dared it to ring while she dragged the boxes from her office into the living room, unearthed a roll of duct tape to seal them up, and then headed for the bedroom again to start packing her suitcase. Nothing like having an organized mind. With five things to do she could usually manage to get through two before she started skipping, wandering all over the map. It was something else she was working on. Efficiency.

"Oops—call Doris," she reminded herself.

Davonda came by just as she finished packing. "Going somewhere?" she inquired, eyeing the suitcase beside the front door.

"Just for a day or so. Research."

"Research, hmm? Then why're you blushing?"

"Oh, for heaven's sake, if my face is red it's from exertion. I've been handling those boxes of…of research material."

"Umm-hmm. If you say so, girl. Just watch it, y'hear? You're nowhere near as smart as you think you are."

"Just because you went to Yale and I didn't." It was a standing joke between them, Davonda's degrees and Lily's lack of even a GED, and their relative income levels.

"Okay, I've made a few changes. Look 'em over, call if you've got any questions, otherwise initial where I did, sign 'em and I'll pick it up…when?"

"When what? Oh. The contract."

A three-book contract with a seven-figure advance, that's all. At any other time in her life she'd be dancing on the rooftops. At the moment she seemed to have blown all her emotional fuses. "Tell you what, I'll take it with me and read it over word by word and drop it in the mail in case I'm gone more than a couple of days, okay?'' She wouldn't be, but just in case...

"Who is he? No, don't answer that, I don't even want to know. But, girl, you know the score.'' Davonda knew more about Lily's past than anyone other than the counselor who had straightened her out and set her on a more constructive path.

"Honestly, Davie, it's just research. I came across some fascinating material, only it's—well, it's complicated.''

"Complicated. Right.'' Davonda rolled her expressive eyes. "At least the timing's good. Best thing in the world—get out of town until things settle down around here. Then if you want to sue the phone company, I'll represent you.''

Not until she was standing under the shower did it occur to Lily that the fire she was leaping into might be more dangerous than the frying pan she was leaping out of. While hot water drilled down on the tense muscles at the back of her neck and sluiced down her body, she thought about that crazy prickle of awareness that had come over her the first time she'd seen Curt Powers at the bookstore.

She let the water run cool and then cold. It didn't help. Words and phrases popped into her mind as she visualized the way he walked. Snake-hipped. Tigerlike. Gliding, as though he had a case of dynamite balanced on his head.

She shut off the water and shivered, not from the cold so much as from the awareness that always served as a warning. The awareness of her own femininity. Of what she had denied for so long, but hadn't quite managed to kill. That she was a woman with a woman's needs. A woman afraid to allow anyone to come too close, because closeness meant getting hurt, and she'd been hurt too often ever to risk it again.

"Face it, girl, you're a fraud. Clear case of early malnutrition. Your body grew up, but your brain barely made it past puberty." Here she had her first three-book contract with a seven-figure advance, with a creep making her life a living hell, and all she could think about was what sex would be like with a man she didn't know, didn't trust and certainly didn't like. A lion of a man into whose den she had just delivered herself.

A lion of a man? Talk about your purple prose.

But it was true. Whatever it was that men had that made women do incredibly stupid things, Curt Powers had cornered the market. Testosterone? Machismo?

Whatever. Chemistry was another area where she was woefully ignorant.

"And, Bess, he's not even handsome, not by male-cover-model standards. Remind me to tell you about the covers we have these days." She dusted down with lilac-scented talcum powder, sneezed twice and muttered, "Bless you." She didn't know if self-blessings counted, but she needed all the help she could get.

"Did women have biological clocks in your day, Bess? I've been reading up on it, and you know what? I'm beginning to believe it's more than just a medical myth."

What if he tried to seduce her, she wondered as she brushed her teeth. Would raging hormones overcome common sense? Where did temptation fit in? Because she was tempted. She didn't have to like him—she didn't even have to know him, to be tempted.

What if she tried to seduce him? She knew how it was done on paper. On paper, she had done it plenty of times. Even though her books fell into the category of suspense, there was always an element of romance involved. And while personally she went out of her way to avoid temptation, she knew all about it. Even a hardheaded realist could dream. It was those very dreams that enabled her to do what she did, which was to create lovely, sexy, temporarily dangerous, but eventually happy-ever-after lives for other people to live.

Curt Powers was the kind of man she wrote about in her books and avoided like the plague in real life. She would be safe, she reminded herself as she rinsed and spat, just as long as she remembered the rules. Rule number one, know the odds going in.

Too late, she was already in. She grimaced at the face in the mirror and skipped to rule number two. Run like hell. That was still a possibility. And if worse came to worst, she would have to rely on thumbs, knees, teeth and five-alarm screams.

At nine-thirty the next morning she took one look at the mess stacked in her living room and headed for the medicine cabinet. Somebody had evidently borrowed her head for basketball practice. Either that or she had a bad case of coffee jitters. She kept meaning to swear off caffeine. Kept forgetting to do it.

After three aspirin, washed down with last night's stale coffee, she stood in front of her closet and pondered what to wear. One of the skills she was working on was how to dress appropriately for the occasion. Things had been easier back when she'd worn whatever she could swipe from other people's clotheslines. Now she fought a constant battle between her personal desire for anonymity and her publisher's insistence on exposure. They'd even given her a Web page, for gosh sake, and she wasn't even online. Lily the writer wore silks and strappy high heels. The real Lily dressed down. Way down.

She opted for baggy slacks, a man's shirts, and a pair

of sneakers—the discount store variety, not the name brand. This was a working trip, not a publicity tour.

"You trying to prove something, Lily?" she asked, all innocence.

"Damn right I am!" she growled back at the mirror.

And that was another thing—she'd have to try to remember not to talk to herself while she was at Powers Point. At least not out loud. And definitely not to talk to Bess.

He was early. Her doorbell rang at one minute to ten. Armor firmly in place, Lily opened the door, silently daring him to comment on her baggy eyes, her baggy slacks or any other bags he happened to notice.

"Rough night?" He noticed, all right.

"Caffeine," she snapped.

"Right. Any more gifts?"

"I don't want to talk about it."

He lifted his brows in a silent challenge, which she chose to ignore. "It's your choice. Did you tell anyone where you were going?"

"Well, sure I did. I called the president, and he said he'd have the FBI and the CIA keep an eye on my underwear drawer." She wished she'd taken the time to camouflage the shadows under her eyes. Knowing she looked like hell gave him the advantage. "Could we just get this show on the road?"

Something about the way he was looking at her made her regret her attitude. If she didn't know better, she might even believe he cared. Another thing she wasn't very good at was apologies, but she felt compelled to give it a shot. "I'm not at my best early in the morning, okay?"

He glanced pointedly at his watch. It was one of those ugly ones with all the bells and whistles that did everything but tie your shoelaces for you. She'd had one once, but she'd never been able to figure out how to set it.

They were standing there by a ton of stuff that was going to have to be dragged downstairs and loaded into her car. Sleep deprived or not, if they didn't get moving she was going to lose her nerve, and then she'd be right back where she started—stuck with all the flakes, weirdos and other vermin. Her stress level registered at least a 6.8 on whatever scale such things were measured by. No wonder he was looking at her as if he didn't know whether to run or throw a hammerlock on her. She could have told him that he himself was a large part of the problem.

Trouble was, he was also a part of the solution—at least on a temporary basis.

He smelled of shaving cream. Not cologne, but plain old, drugstore shave cream. Gold watches, tasseled loafers, heavy cologne and Italian suits she could have handled easily. Clean, rumpled khakis, faded black knit shirts, ancient deck shoes on a plain, unadorned male might be a little harder to deal with.

"Look, are we going or not? I have to be back by the end of the week to start on a new proposal."

He shrugged as if to say it was her call. Which it was. And then he reached for the box on the top of the stack, winced and set it down again.

"I've got a handcart there beside the sofa."

"I wondered how you managed to get this stuff up here."

"I'm not exactly stupid," she told him. He looked as if he might argue the point, but instead, he slid the top box off onto the handcart, then reached for the next one.

Lily took one last look around inside, thought of all the reasons to go and all the reasons not to. It was the promise to Bess that tipped the scales.

Sure it was. A promise to a woman who's been dead for at least a century. And you think you're sane? Forget it, Lily, your last marble just rolled down the storm drain.

They took the elevator. Lily preferred the stairs, having an aversion to small, enclosed spaces, but she could hardly ask the man to hump the heavy cart down three flights, then return for the rest of the boxes. They'd left four of them outside her door, along with her suitcase. She had her laptop and her canvas tote with her. The tote was never out of sight. It was her survival kit.

"Stand guard over this one while I get the rest."

She opened her mouth to argue, then shut it again. "This is a very safe neighborhood," she replied, and he just looked at her. No words needed.

"Safer than most, anyway," she called after him as he disappeared inside the old brick apartment house. Something was definitely wrong with his leg. Or maybe his back. He didn't like elevators any better than she did; didn't much care for stairs, either, but he wasn't about to let on. Self-confidence was one thing. Pigheadedness was another. She wasn't yet sure into which category Powers fell, but she had a feeling she'd soon find out.

"You do have juice, don't you?" she asked when the rest of the load had been relayed outside to the parking area.

"Juice?"

"You know, electricity?"

Except for his eyes, his expression remained unchanged. Lily could almost swear it was amusement she saw lurking in the dark-blue depths. Lord help her if the man had a sense of humor. She could resist almost anything but that.

"I've got juice." He swung the first box up into the back of his pickup, grimaced and reached for the next one. She said, "We could fit all six boxes in my car if we put two in the trunk, three in the back seat and one in the passenger seat." She'd insisted on driving her own car. He hadn't argued.

"What, you don't trust me?"

"The last man I trusted was Santa Claus. I pretty much lost faith when Santa got stoned and forgot what day of the year it was." Clamping her lips shut, she thought, why didn't I use that duct tape on my mouth instead of the boxes?

"We'll haul 'em in my truck."

Lily took one last look at the old brick building, the first place she had ever truly thought of as home. For months she had practically camped out here, refusing to buy anything but the bare necessities in case her luck changed and she had to go back to scrounging to make ends meet. A writer's income, she'd quickly learned, came in spurts, if at all.

But her luck had not only held, it had continued to improve. Gradually she had dropped her guard and settled in. First she had bought plants. Next she'd furnished her office. Then she'd bought a faded, but beautiful, old fake Oriental rug, had bookshelves built and quickly filled them. Other touches—chairs and tables—had been added each time she finished a book. The antique doll, a few small, inexpensive paintings, each one representing another small triumph. Until recently it had been her haven, her reward, her favorite place in the world.

"Ready to ride?"

She lifted her chin and tilted her head slightly, the way the photographer had showed her the last time she'd had publicity shots done. It was supposed to imply self-confidence imbued with a hint of mystery. The real mystery was why she was doing this. As for self-confidence...

"Ready to ride," she said.

Four

Curt handed her a map in case they got separated in traffic. "Just follow the course I've marked, watch for the turnoff onto Highway 12 to Hatteras, and keep going until you come to the bridge. I'll wait there for you."

"Follow the yellow-marked road? Is that a bit of whimsy? I'd never have suspected it." If her tone sounded mocking, it was sheer bravado.

Ignoring the remark, Curt watched her slide on a pair of dark glasses, the kind that marked her immediately as someone to notice, and wondered if he'd have been smarter to write off his losses and forget the whole thing. Was thirty-six old enough for a midlife crisis? Senility?

Granted, he'd hung on longer than most men in his line of work, but he could have sworn his brain had still been functioning. Evidently it had been deep-sixed right along with his diving career.

Headed south on Highway 168, Curt dealt with a number of second thoughts. The Powers papers were now in his possession. They were rightfully his. He could lose Ms. Fancy-Pants on the way south, cut her out of the deal entirely, possession being nine-tenths of the law.

No, he couldn't. He could be a real bastard when he had to, but his integrity had never been called into question. So he would deal with the situation, share what he felt like sharing and ignore the fact that the lady got under his skin quicker than a whole herd of chiggers.

By now she was probably having a few second thoughts of her own. She hadn't struck him as the kind of woman who would follow a strange man home, but then, what did he know about women? He'd proved his lack of expertise. He was willing to give her the benefit of the doubt, considering the situation she was in. Under heavy stress, common sense was often the first casualty. For all he knew she might be after something besides what was in those boxes. It wouldn't be the first time a woman had come on to him sexually when they'd learned what he was. Being a SEAL was a turn-on for a certain type of woman.

It would have been funny if it weren't so damned pathetic. Any man less dangerous would be hard to find. If that's what Lady Lily had in mind, then she was in for a disappointment. A quick one-night stand was out of the question. *Anything* quick was out of the question.

As for anything more protracted, experience had taught him that a man who suddenly drops out of sight for months at a time with no notice is a poor risk when it comes to intimate personal relationships.

Lily, following the tailgate of that monstrous silver pickup truck, wondered if menopause could set in at the age of twenty-eight. She'd put it down to an overload of stress, but it could be hormonal. "It's only a business trip," she reassured herself. "It's even tax deductible."

She had a feeling there might be more involved, but this was no time for second thoughts. If she'd been layering a plot, she'd have limited herself on the complications. But she wasn't, and she couldn't, and so she settled for justifying—for rationalizing.

Getting out of town was a good idea. She'd be seeing a different area, and as a writer, it couldn't hurt to broaden her horizon. But the most compelling reason of all was that she would be sleeping in the same house—maybe even the same room—where Bess had once slept. If she opened herself up to the experience, and she was good at doing that, she could not only tell Bess's story, she might even be able to generate enough material that she could try her hand at writing historical suspense.

Lily drove confidently and well, and occasionally too fast, but not today. She had too much on her mind to risk getting pulled over. In scrambling out of harm's way, she had knowingly, deliberately put herself in the way of a different kind of harm. For her, that was a first.

Under the hypnotic spell of the road, she let her mind wander. What did he think of her? Just because she wrote about man-woman relationships, men occasionally got the idea that she was easy. She wasn't easy. What she was, was impossible. If Curt Powers tried anything, he would discover that, while she might not look it, she could easily handle a man who moved as if every bone in his body had been broken and mended with masking tape.

No matter how sexually attractive he was.

And he was that, all right. Funny, how quickly he'd sneaked in under her guard. As a rule the first thing she did when she found a man attractive was to remind herself of what could happen when a woman let a man get too close. Case in point, her own mother. Once, after another unsuccessful attempt to get herself straightened out, her mother had told her that she'd run away from home at the age of fourteen, ended up on the streets, pregnant, hooked on drugs and scared out of her gourd. "Don't go that road, baby. Don't ever let a man use you, no matter what he promises in return. You're better than that. You're the only decent thing in my life."

It hadn't lasted long, her mother's attempt to get off the stuff. The experts said it was never too late, but for some people, at some point, it was. Lily had managed to escape the trap. She'd done a lot of things she wasn't proud of, but she'd survived and managed to climb out of the hole, up to where the air was clean and fresh and sweet smelling. She didn't do drugs, she didn't smoke, she didn't drink. Even a glass of wine was off-limits. As for men, while she might fantasize—might even poke a toe in the waters, enjoying the occasional dinner date with a man who didn't attract her physically—this was the first time she had ever knowingly, deliberately, exposed herself to a man who affected her not only physically but mentally.

"Bess, you'd damn well better stick with me. I have a feeling this time I might need help."

He was waiting at the Oregon Inlet Bridge. When she'd asked for a street address in case they got separated, he'd told her there was no street, much less a house number. "Cross the inlet, head south until you come to a village. Keep on going until there's nothing in sight but water, dunes and some scrubby vegetation. When you come to an unpainted house with a cemetery on one side and a few ramshackle outbuildings in the back, that's Powers Point. On second thought, just meet me at Oregon Inlet and I'll lead you there."

While he waited, Curt was wondering if he had picked up his socks off the living room floor. Or taken the garbage out before he left. He wondered belatedly about the condition of his guest quarters. The last thing he'd expected when he'd headed north was that he'd be bringing someone home with him. He wasn't what you might call a people person. Never had been. Hell, he even went out of his way to buy groceries in the middle of the night, when there were fewer people around. He collected his mail when he happened to think of it. Most of it was junk mail, which didn't make it worth any extra effort. Which, come to think of it, was what had gotten him in trouble in the first place.

So okay—the house was no showplace. So he might have left a few unwashed dishes. No big deal. If Ms. O'Malley turned up her elegant nose at him, his house, and his lifestyle, it was no big deal. Hell, he didn't even have a lifestyle.

At least he had a life. For a while it had been touch and go. Style could wait until he figured out what he was going to do with the rest of it. Stay in or get out.

Three days, tops, he promised himself as he watched her signal a right turn and pull off the road. He would give her three days to go through his stuff, take whatever notes she wanted to take, and leave. He waited until she got out of her car to ease himself out of the high cab. He should've been walking around, working the kinks out while he waited. He should've worn his back brace, too, but then he didn't always do what was good for him. So he sauntered over to meet her—at least he tried to think of walking carefully so as not to jar anything loose as sauntering. "If you need to use the head, there's one here at the marina. Another one a few miles down the road at Pea Island."

"Is that the wildlife sanctuary? I read about it in last

Sunday's paper. I'd rather stop there if you don't mind. I hope you haven't been waiting long."

"Not at all," he assured her. He might be a physical wreck, but even wrecks had their pride. Waiting for her to look her fill around the busy marina, he couldn't help but admire the way the sun highlighted her cheekbones and the long line of her throat. She wasn't precisely pretty. Forehead too high, nose too proud, cheekbones too pronounced. Patrician was a word that came to mind. He kind of thought it might apply here, and wondered for the first time about her background.

Whatever it was, it had to be a hell of a lot more impressive than his own.

"Let's move on," she said. Stretching her arms out behind her, she flexed her shoulders. "I'm eager to get to Bess's house, to see if I can pick up anything from the ambience."

"If it's vibes you're looking for, you might have to put up with some interference. The house is still pretty much the same, or so I've been told, but a lot's changed on the island since the early days. Tourists, for one thing. The bridge, the highway—surfers and wall-to-wall fishermen." He nodded toward the nearby inlet, where sportsmen of all types, both in and out of boats, vied for space. "Hell, they even moved the lighthouse."

She nodded. He could almost see her taking mental notes. He led the way, pulling into the state-sanctioned rest stop at Pea Island, with its state-sanctioned gift shop and nature trail. He hoped she didn't plan on doing any birdwatching. As usual he planned to get the job done and get out. Or in this case, open the boxes, take what he wanted and let her have the rest.

One thing he definitely looked forward to was being under his own roof, in his own bed, with all the doors and windows wide open. A couple of nights in an airless motel was about all he could take. The food had been pretty good, but then, one of the things he'd been intending to do was to learn how to cook something besides bacon and eggs. His mother had been a lousy cook. Made a botch of her first marriage, too. Evidently, he'd inherited his lack of domestic genes from her side of the family.

While he waited for Lily to emerge, he considered the irony of going this far for a bunch of family records. For a guy who'd been a rolling stone ever since he'd graduated from high school, it was a switch. Suddenly he was a home owner. It sounded a little too much like having an anchor slung around his neck. Still, for the time being, he had nothing better to do than to explore his so-called legacy. Leaning against the hot metal side of the truck, absorbing the sun and salt air, he told himself that if he didn't watch it, he'd be soon planting flowers and hanging curtains at the windows.

He was still there when Lily emerged. Breathing deeply—or as deeply as he dared—of the clean salt air, he watched a pair of white herons lift off, admiring their graceful lines. Reluctantly he admired Lily's lines, too. He liked the way she moved, as if she knew precisely where she was going. With the wind pressing her loose shirt and slacks against her body, she managed to look fragile, feminine and resilient at the same time.

Hell of a thing. The woman could tick him off, turn him on and mess up his mind without even trying. And here he was, taking her home with him. The medics just might have been right when they'd warned him about discharging himself from the hospital too soon. Evidently, a few parts of his body were recovering faster than others.

Just don't start anything you can't finish, Powers.

They headed south. Curt was scowling when they left

Pea Island, grimacing with pain by the time they pulled into what passed for his driveway. He parked over in the sand, leaving the narrow stretch of marl to her. That toy car of hers wasn't cut out for sand driving. Pausing a moment before easing himself out of the high cab, he took in the now-familiar surroundings. House, outbuildings, tombstones and what was left of an ancient wharf down on the marshy edge of the Pamlico Sound.

Stark was the word that came to mind here. If the weathered frame house that had obviously been added onto at random had ever boasted a lick of paint, there was no sign of it now. The whole thing sloped slightly to the northeast. There were a few sections of picket fence still standing, one on the ground. A few rusty strands of barbed wire curled uselessly around some freestanding posts.

Well, hell, he hadn't promised her a rose garden.

"This looks…interesting."

She'd come up behind him and caught him off guard, one more indication that he'd lost his edge. Whether or not he decided to take early retirement, he would do well not to forget his training.

"I'll carry your gear inside," he said gruffly. "The boxes can wait until after I open up."

The inside was no better than the outside. He didn't even know if the bed in the other room was dry. When he'd first moved in, everything inside had felt damp, smelled of mice and mildew, which wasn't too surprising in a house that had been boarded up for a couple of years. The key he'd been given wouldn't work, and rather than break in he'd driven down to Avon, the nearest village to the south, and made a few inquiries.

He'd located an old friend of his father's who had told him he'd boarded up the windows and put on new padlocks after the house had been broken into a few times.

"There weren't much left to steal. I reckon kids took whatever they could haul off. I'm real sorry about that. Me and your daddy sort of lost touch."

You and me, both, Curt had wanted to say but hadn't. He'd opened up the place and let the wind blow through while a local carpenter made basic repairs. Once it was habitable, he'd moved in.

Marginally habitable, he amended now, watching the woman who looked as out of place as a pig at a tea party. Elegant, sexy and windblown, she was trying hard not to show her dismay.

"There's a pretty decent motel not too far from here. I can call and see if they have a vacancy," he offered hopefully.

"No, thanks, this is fine. I'm pretty sure Bess didn't stay at any motel."

She had a way of smiling that started in her eyes, then tugged at the corners of her mouth. Curt found himself smiling back before he thought better of it. Quickly switching to a scowl, he led the way to the guest room. "Probably needs airing out. There's some linens in the closet on the shelf. I'll make your bed for you."

"Thanks, but that won't be necessary."

Relieved, he nodded. His back didn't take kindly to the thought of any more bending and stretching. But God, the place was a dump. The bed sagged, the ticking was stained, the mattress one of those cotton-filled ones that looked about as comfortable as a bushel bag of potatoes. There was a three-legged dresser against one wall, with all five drawers stuck tight. He'd tried to open them when he'd first moved in. Hadn't bothered since. For the short time he planned to be here, he didn't need the storage, and besides, he didn't particularly care to invade the privacy of any nesting mice.

The room's only chair had once been varnished, but was now blotched with whitish stains. It was ugly. Everything in the house was ugly. Seeing her standing there, in her black slacks and white silk shirt, he suddenly felt like swearing for no real reason except that by contrast, she pointed up the bleakness of his own life.

"Look, you can have the other bedroom. At least it's dry. I'll put on clean sheets, but I'd better warn you in case you're a late sleeper, the morning sun comes barreling in through the window like a five-alarm fire. You might've noticed I don't have shades or curtains."

"This is fine. The view's nice, and if you have a board I can put between the springs and the mattress, it'll be perfect. I don't care for a soft bed."

"You mean a sagging bed."

"That, too," she admitted with another of those half shy smiles that came and went almost too fast to register.

Curt slid his hands down his hips, hooked his thumbs under his belt and tried to remember if there was any scrap lumber left over from the roof repairs. If not, he'd rip a few boards off one of the sheds. He really didn't want to give up his own bed—not that he wouldn't be willing to share.

Not that sharing would do him any good.

First thing he'd done when he moved in was to send off for a good, firm mattress. He'd still worn a back brace then. On damp days he had occasionally been forced to resort to using use his crutch, but he'd tossed both items after the first week. The medic had given him pain pills which he'd refused to take until a nurse had explained that if he truly enjoyed being miserable, that was up to him, but the pills were supposed to reduce the inflammation and speed up the healing process.

Good thing he'd been in peak physical condition when

the SDV had bought it, else his body might not have been able to stand the compression. As it was, he'd got off easy. A few broken ribs, a few burns—a blown eardrum, a compromised lung, along with some nasty bugs he'd picked up from spending all that time buried up to his neck in stinking river mud. He was dealing with it. With that and the guilt that went along with being the lone survivor.

With her room aired out, her sagging bed reinforced and spread with clean, if musty-smelling linens, Lily looked around for a place to set up her computer. "All I need is a corner with a small shelf and a chair," she said. "Maybe a card table? You did say the power here was reliable, didn't you?"

Curt's stomach growled. It had occurred to him that he was probably expected to feed her as long as she was sharing his roof. Hell of a note. "Computer?" he repeated.

"That thing with the screen and the keyboard?" she reminded him.

"Oh. Yeah." Could her hair possibly be as soft as it looked? The last woman whose hair he had touched had been bleached, curled and sprayed. Definitely not touch tempting.

"I guess you could set up in my office for as long as you'll be here," he said reluctantly. It was hardly likely they'd both be working at the same time. He worked whenever he couldn't sleep, which was a portion of almost every night.

So he showed her into the room he called an office. "I'll slide this stuff over. You can set up your equipment on this end, plug into the back-up power supply and I'll rig another light."

The single overhead bulb was hardly sufficient. He used a clip-on with a drop cord, but a hotshot lady novelist probably had fancier requirements. The room was small. He figured it had once been a back bedroom, but there was no way to know for sure. Not that it mattered.

Even setting up, they were in each other's way. Each time he brushed past, shifting the stacks of papers, files he'd been meaning to organize and back up on disks when he had the time, he was aware all over again of the dangers of getting involved with a woman like Lily O'Malley.

With any woman at all. But O'Malley was particularly dangerous because he had only to look at her body to find himself wanting to know more about it—wanting to explore at leisure every dark, sweet secret she possessed. Had only to look into her eyes to be captured by something he saw there, something he sensed just under the surface. For a lady who had Back Off, Buster, written all over her, she seemed curiously vulnerable.

Oh, yeah, she was a puzzle. She was a challenge, and he'd never been able to resist a challenge, which was why he'd gone into the line of work he had.

But this one he was determined to resist if it killed him. He was in no position to do anything else.

Five

A slight breeze had stirred sluggishly all day. Just before sunset, it sighed out, leaving the air hot and humid. The kind of air that steals energy and replaces it with temper. Left to himself, Curt would have stripped down, crossed the stretch of burning sand to the ocean and hit the surf. The therapist had recommended water aerobics. He was pretty sure body surfing fell in that category. If it didn't kill him, it would probably cure him…eventually.

"I don't suppose you have an air conditioner," Lily said wistfully. There was a gleam of sweat on her skin that made him want to lick it off. He put the aberration down to the weather and wondered if it was worth getting the place rewired to handle some heavy-duty cooling for as long as he planned to be here.

"Sorry. No AC, no stereo, no TV." In other words, no distractions and damned few comforts. At the moment he could have done with a distraction.

"How do you keep up with the news?"

"Shortwave radio. Internet."

Her mouth formed a silent O. No lipstick, just Lily. Did she realize what a turn-on naked lips were on a woman with skin like hers? He figured there must be some interesting genes in her pool. Italian. Maybe Far Eastern or American Indian.

The name, though, was strictly Irish. If it really was her name. It was probably a pen name. A pseudonym. Honesty was a quality he'd learned not to expect in a woman.

On the other hand, a lily by any other name and all that...

"Hey, it's suppertime, isn't it?" he exclaimed, feigning cheerfulness.

This wasn't going to work. He wasn't interested in food, he was interested in woman. In this woman in particular. He didn't trust her. He didn't know her. He had no idea if he would like her or not if he ever got to know her, because he had no intention of getting to know her any better than he did. They had one thing in common, and one thing only.

Two, if you counted hunger. Her stomach growled, as if on cue.

She looked embarrassed, but carried it off beautifully. "Food would be lovely," she said politely.

"So...what's your pleasure, madam? Pizza? Seafood?" He knew what his would be under more favorable circumstances, the lady being willing.

"Whatever you like is fine with me. Naturally, I intend to pay my share."

It was just past five, but he'd skipped lunch. If she'd wanted to stop she could've asked. She hadn't.

"It's not a case of paying your share, it's a case of what kind of takeout do you want, pizza or seafood?"

"That's it?"

"They deliver. Others might. I haven't tried anything else."

"What about dining out?"

"Help yourself. I'm planning on ordering in, but I'll give you directions if you'd rather explore a few of the local establishments." Nice going, Powers. Show her what a classy guy you are. "Look, I'm sorry—tomorrow I'll do better, I promise, but for now, can we just make this easy?"

Oh, hell, he was begging.

Trouble was, he was stiff and sore after being cooped up inside the cab of his truck all day and then lugging in those blasted boxes. All he really wanted to do was fill his belly, then stand under a hot shower for about twenty minutes until he'd washed away some of the accumulated stiffness. He felt about a hundred years old.

No way he was going to admit it, though.

"Pizza's fine with me." She smiled at him. She had the kind of smile that could kick a guy in the gut and cut off his air supply before he realized what had hit him.

He'd already been that route.

"I'll call it in." He reached for the phone, relieved at the easy victory.

This is not going to work, he told himself again as he sank into one of the room's two chairs and punched in the number of his favorite dining establishment. "What do you like on yours?" he asked.

While he waited for someone to pick up on the other end and waited for her to make up her mind what she wanted, he studied the way her hands moved. Small, graceful gestures. Nothing fluttery. "Hi, Sal, make it two tonight. Yeah, my usual and..." He shot her a questioning look.

Her face took on a dreamy expression. "Hmm…extra cheese? And how about black olives, anchovies and banana peppers?"

He passed it on, listened to Sal's comment on the lousy fishing and hung up. "So what would you like to drink with that—beer?" She had claimed the other chair, a lopsided, leather-covered recliner that had evidently been too heavy to steal. Long legs straight out in front of her, ankles crossed, she rested her hands, palms up, on her thighs and closed her eyes. She looked bushed, but then, neither of them had gotten much sleep lately, what with one thing and another. A miserable motel bed on his part, plus the kind of dreams that left him needy and frustrated.

On her part there'd been the phone calls and someone messing around in her panty drawer. The phone calls alone would be enough to send most women into a full-blown case of hysterics. Ms. O'Malley was pretty cool, if you didn't count deliberately helping herself to someone else's private property and then trying to get away with it on the basis of being a writer.

Maybe it was a celebrity thing. The I'm-somebody, you're-nobody, you-owe-me syndrome. He'd known a few celebrities, mostly sports figures. A minor movie star. The players earned their status. The starlet couldn't act her way out of a paper bag, but she was drop-dead gorgeous. O'Malley would never make it as a starlet.

Funny thing, though—he had a growing sense that underneath all the hoopla, she was a very private person. Or would like to be. He hadn't yet made up his mind whether she was plain or beautiful—it all depended on a man's idea of beauty. Up to now his had been pretty standard. Long legs, big boobs, blond hair, blue eyes.

Lily had the legs, but fell short in all other categories.

Her eyes were gray, her hair was richer than black, darker than brown. As for her breasts...

He cut short the inventory. For the next couple of days they'd be sharing meals, sharing work space and his small, no-frills bathroom. Other than the contents of those six battered cartons, that was *all* they were going to share.

Opening a pair of shadowed gray eyes, Lily said wistfully, "I don't suppose you have any milk."

"I could drive down and get some." The thought of climbing back into his truck nearly threw his back into spasms.

"No, don't do that." Her smile faded and with it, the last hint of color in her wan face.

We're a pair, all right, he thought. Too tired to fight, too proud to admit defeat. Another thing they had in common. If she'd been one of those terminally cheerful types, he'd have walked out the back door and kept on going.

Correction: if she'd been one of those, he'd never have brought her here in the first place. "How about evaporated? I keep a can on hand for emergency use."

She came at him again with that wisp of a smile. He really wished she wouldn't do it, because it made him forget temporarily that this was strictly a business deal, no more, no less. They weren't friends. If anything, they were competitors. Not even friendly competitors.

In spite of his doubts, things went surprisingly smoothly. Curt went out of his way not to invade her personal space, and Lily returned the favor. He should have been satisfied. Instead, he found himself prowling through his house, needing to know where she was in order to avoid her.

Ironically, the more unobtrusive she tried to be, the more impossible she was to ignore. Half the time she was sprawled on the porch with a couple of those old diaries, a pen behind her ear and a notepad in her lap, staring out over the water, so still he'd thought she was asleep the first few times he'd seen her there. Stillness, not to mention silence, were not qualities he associated with women.

At least not with any of the women he'd ever known— including his mother.

One of the first things she'd done after breakfast that second morning was visit the cemetery. Knelt and tried to read names and dates. Actually took a rubbing off one. He was curious to know why, but refused to ask. He'd walked out there a time or two himself when he'd first moved in, studying the few stones that were still legible. Most of them were worn nearly smooth. Sandblasted. One had fallen over. He'd meant to set it upright when he felt up to digging a base for it, but he'd never got around to it.

He wished now that he had. Whoever they were, they were obviously related to him, the Powers name being predominant. There was one Elizabeth Bagby. As the name hadn't rung any bells, he'd dismissed it. His father's grave was there—the newest stone, looking somehow lonely among all those ancient markers.

Damn. This was getting too close, too personal. He might've done better to toss the deed, the boxes—the whole lot and go somewhere new. Maybe even back to Oklahoma. At least cornfields and oil rigs didn't mess up his mind.

It was on the third day that she asked him if he knew who was who in the graveyard. She'd spent the morning sitting cross-legged out there under a scalding sun, notebook in hand, more often than not staring out over the water. He figured that must be the way writers worked. An hour or so of daydreaming for every line put down on paper.

"All I know is what's carved in stone," he said, and

immediately regretted the flip answer. He was pretty sure one of them must be old Matthew, his great-great-grandfather. As a professional diver, he'd been more interested in the man's ship than in his mortal remains. It seemed irreverent if not downright callous, now that he'd had time to think about it, but the truth was, the only sense of family he had came from those stories his father had told him back when he was almost too young to remember. Stories about ships and the men who sailed them. It was the adventure that had stuck in his mind, not the family thing. His mother had never talked about the man other than that he was gone a lot, and she wasn't cut out to be a grass widow. Over the years Curt had managed to hang on to a few good memories, but he'd kicked out those that gave him that restless, empty feeling.

"Know what? I'm beginning to think the Elizabeth Bagby buried in your cemetery was our Bess. In her later journals she mentions a man named Horace Bagby often enough to be significant. Maybe by the time I leave I'll have put it all together."

It was the first reference she'd made to leaving. Curt knew she had some deadline or another—she'd mentioned it before they'd left Norfolk, which was the only reason he'd reluctantly brought her home with him. He could put up with anything for a couple of days. Hell, he'd gone without food, water and sleep for longer than that. A lot longer.

Trouble was, now that she was here, she didn't seem all that eager to wind things up and get back to where she belonged. If he was honest—and he always tried to be, particularly with himself—Curt was no longer quite so eager to get rid of her. In spite of a deep sense of privacy, he was finding it surprisingly easy to share his personal space. She didn't intrude, she was just…around. The occasional soft-voiced observation—a hint of wildflowers in his john after she'd showered. Mostly, she read all the time, even while they were eating.

During the day when she was outside, wandering around the graveyard or poking around the sound side, he used the time to organize files, reshuffle a few investments and dig into a few more of old Matthew's logbooks. Whatever else he was, the man had been no great hand at keeping records. Manifests, weather observations, personnel matters and standard log entries were all set down together in a bold hand in no particular order.

They shared the front porch whenever there was a breeze off the ocean. Now and then he would read a passage aloud. Or she would. It didn't mean anything—the sharing. They were both reading about the same people, the same era, after all. Still, it was…pleasant. Which was surprising when he thought about it, so mostly he didn't.

Nights were another matter. Tapering off his medications, he'd been cutting the dosage every third day. Which meant he had even more trouble than usual sleeping, only now he didn't feel quite as free to prowl. Not that she did anything overtly to disturb him. Still, knowing there was a woman in bed only a few feet away was hardly conducive to sound sleep. He told himself it wasn't Lily in particular. Under the circumstances, any woman would have had the same effect. A man had certain basic needs, and he'd gone without sex for too long.

The thing was he was beginning to suspect his problem might be a little more complex than a simple need for sexual release. Which was why he reminded himself several times a day that this was strictly business. Strictly a temporary alliance. He cut short the shared reading, tried to keep conversation to a minimum, avoided touching— hell, he even avoided looking whenever he could.

What he hadn't quite mastered was the ability to switch off his brain on command.

What was it they said about the brain? That it was man's largest erogenous zone? The world's greatest aphrodisiac?

Oh, yeah. That he could vouch for.

They'd started out with a plan. That first day, as tired as they'd both been, they had opened all six boxes and made preliminary plans to inventory the contents. The second day Curt had started with the logbooks and miscellaneous loose papers. Each succeeding day had gone more or less the same, with Lily exploring the house and grounds, then settling down with either a diary or one of the travel columns.

Curt waited until she settled and then chose his own spot. If she stayed inside, he went out. If she sat out on the front porch, he kicked back in his living room lounger with a pillow for lumbar support. But then, sooner or later their paths would cross. She would pour iced tea and join him wherever he happened to be. If she'd started chattering, he'd have walked away, but she never did. She spoke now and then in that soft, slightly husky voice of hers with the unidentifiable accent, but mostly she said nothing.

Restful woman.

Restful in some ways, he amended. Damned unsettling in others.

"What do you hope to discover in all those old logbooks?" she asked when they met in the kitchen to put together a couple of sandwiches on the fifth day.

"Whatever's there. Maybe what happened to the *Black Swan*. Mustard or mayo?"

"Mustard, please. I can't get over Bess. She's really fascinating. I'm pretty sure she was less than truthful at times, but then, a woman uses whatever weapons she has."

Barefoot, dressed in baggy white pants and a man's blue cotton shirt, she reached past him to add another layer of banana peppers to her sandwich, took a big bite and groaned with pleasure. He'd noticed that about her, too. There was nothing delicate about her appetite. Which made him wonder whether or not...

The hell it did.

"Actually, from the travel articles, I get a feeling she seldom told the truth when a lie would suffice."

Curt had read a few of the travel pieces, too. The Central American ones, in particular. Unless the region had changed one hell of a lot in the past hundred years or so—not out of the question, by any means—then damn right, she lied. And while he wouldn't come right out and say so, he went so far as to ask, "Have you seen any boa constrictors or wildcats around here? According to the piece she did about Powers Point, they're as common as green flies."

Lily nearly choked. Curt whacked her between the shoulder blades "You're kidding. Real wildcats?"

"Read it yourself."

"Jeeze Louise," she murmured reverently, and he had to grin at the lady wordsmith's ability to express herself.

There was only room for two ice trays in the antique refrigerator. Lily emptied one in her jar of iced tea, refilled it and carefully replaced it. The compressor came on with a whining protest. Thing should've been retired fifty years ago.

Popping the cap on his beer, Curt added a new refrigerator to his mental shopping list. When he was ready to move on, any improvements would only jack up the resale value. Meanwhile, it wouldn't hurt to add a few creature comforts.

But not until Lily left. He didn't want to make her any

more comfortable than she already was. Still, he had to admit she handled roughing it pretty well. For a woman. If she didn't like the setup, she kept it to herself, to the point where he actually went out of his way to provoke her at least once a day. He got a kick out of the cracks in her ladylike facade—the contrast between that polite little voice and the don't-tread-on-me attitude she had raised to the level of a fine art. The more he came to know her, the more convinced he was that something about her didn't add up. If there was one thing his years of training had taught him, it was that appearances could be—and usually were—deceiving.

She had tried to get away with something that belonged to him, he reminded himself. That was just one of the things that bugged him. The fact that while he had a moral claim she had a legal claim only muddied the waters. And then there was this business with Bess. Whose relative was she, anyway?

It wasn't even as if he cared about the damn papers that much—at least he hadn't started out caring. But the more he read, the more he was beginning to understand why he hadn't been satisfied to stay in Oklahoma for the rest of his life and grow corn.

Lily's obsession was a little harder to figure. She claimed some kind of kinship with Bess, on account of they were both women and both writers. But then, unless he was mistaken, there had been any number of successful female writers through the ages. Why Bess in particular? Lily admitted that she'd never heard of the woman before, much less any of her novels.

The Virgin and the Vengeful Groom by E. Powers?

Give me a break.

They were sitting out on the porch, sharing a slight breeze and the last of their sandwiches. Lily, idly pushing

her rocking chair with one foot, was frowning down at one
of the older diaries. "Hmm," she murmured. Held the
book up to the light and frowned at it some more.

"Found something interesting?" There happened to be
a speck of mustard at the corner of her mouth that he found
a lot more interesting than the chart he'd been trying to
decipher.

"I'm not sure. Her handwriting was never great, but in
these earlier diaries, it was truly execrable. I wonder what
her mama did about schooling."

"Execrable. Does that mean what I think it does?"

Lily glanced up, captured by his remarkable eyes. They
were an unusual shade of dark-blue, hard to read even for
someone who was good at it. At the moment they held a
definite twinkle. So far she had never heard him laugh and
had only seen his smile once or twice. He even teased with
a straight face. It was a disarming trait.

"Probably. As euphemisms go, it's pretty expressive,"
she said dryly.

"Means not so good, huh?"

"You got it." She grinned, then stretched, yawned and
begged his pardon. They'd both been up since shortly after
daybreak, finding it easier to do as much as possible before
the heat and humidity grew too oppressive. The late-
afternoon breeze was a bonus, but even the breeze was
hot, damp and enervating. "Take this word right here..."
Leaning over, she pointed out a short series of loops and
swoops. "Do you have any idea what it could be? Is this
an *R* or an *N*?"

"Looks like an *R*...that first one's a *C*."

"Hmm. Then it must be crow, not wren." Her arm
brushed against his, and she held her breath. She was going
to have to do a better job of keeping her distance. Not easy
to do when her insides were so unsettled. At first she'd

thought it was the water. Now she was beginning to suspect it was the man. She'd been having some wild dreams lately, waking up with all sorts of vague longings.

Oh, it was the man, all right. She wasn't all that stupid. She might lack experience, but she certainly didn't lack knowledge. When he went on to say, "Crow's nest, to be more precise," she actually shivered. Well, damn. Even his voice brought on a physical reaction.

A little breathlessly she said, "I'm pretty sure she was no older than, say…twelve when she wrote this. Which means she was still living aboard her father's ship. You're telling me some bird built a nest on a *ship?*"

"The crow's nest is a lookout platform, usually at the top of the highest mast."

"Oh."

While Lily stared down at the book in his hands, Curt stared at the top of her head. The sun brought out reddish glints in her dark hair, loosed the faint scent of wildflowers he'd noticed before. She had two distinct cowlicks. Even more than the rich color, the silken texture and the enticing scent, that small imperfection slipped under his guard.

Quickly looking away, he cleared his throat. "Pretty common term. I'm surprised a famous writer like you wouldn't have recognized it."

"Yes, well, this famous writer still has a few king-size gaps in her education."

"Don't we all," he murmured, surprised and oddly touched that she would admit it. While she wasn't quite as arrogant as he'd first thought, she had more defenses than he would have expected in a successful novelist. "Wanna know my big weakness?" Other than dual cowlicks, that was. "Spelling. No logic to it."

"Sure there is, didn't you ever hear of phonics?"

"Yeah, and I keep wanting to know why it's not spelled the way it's pronounced."

She laughed aloud. He grinned, surprising himself. Probably surprising her even more, from the look on her face. She murmured something about dictionaries and computer spell-checks and went back to wrestling with cramped penmanship, faded ink and archaic wording, and the moment passed.

Unfortunately, his growing fascination didn't. Nor was it likely to unless something happened to relieve the increasing tension. Living with Lily, even on a temporary basis, was turning out to be a major complication in the life he'd been determined to simplify.

You've simplified it, all right, man. Simplified it beyond all comprehension.

They made it through the first five days by tiptoeing carefully past land mines. Curt made a point of not inquiring about her past, her love life or anything of a more personal nature than whether she liked her eggs fried crisp, sunny-side up or mangled.

Lily deliberately refrained from asking about his scars, his sparsely furnished house and why he disliked being shut in as much as she did. Why, instead of buying a window unit and cooling at least one room, he kept all the windows wide open day and night, when it was even hotter outside than it was inside. It hadn't rained since she'd been there, but she had a feeling those windows would stay open, rain or shine.

Not that a little water could do much damage. It was a bare-bones kind of house. She rather liked it. Having experienced every type of domicile from a packing crate in an alley to a rat-infested slum—several of those, in fact— to any number of luxury hotels when she was on tour, she wasn't at all critical. And while she loved her own apartment—her homemade home, as she thought of it—Curt's house had a certain basic appeal. One of the earliest lessons she could remember learning was that what you don't have, you can't lose.

Evidently, she wasn't the only one who felt that way.

Lily never pried, but she had always been observant. It was a useful trait, vital when it came to knowing in advance which way to jump when trouble was headed your way. As a writer, the trait was invaluable. She studied people, tried to work out their motivations, the carrots and sticks that enticed or threatened. It hadn't taken her long to notice that Curt went out of his way to avoid small enclosures and crowds—anyplace where he might find himself cornered. She'd seen that same watchfulness in the eyes of smart cops and smart crooks.

He could be a cop, but she didn't think so. A smart crook would have probably found a more comfortable hideout. One with air-conditioning, at the very least.

The trouble was that she had stopped thinking of him as grist for her writer's mill and started reacting to him as a devastatingly sexy man with a droll sense of humor and far too many shadows behind his lapis-colored eyes. That just might be a problem if she let it become one.

So she wouldn't. She simply wouldn't. Lily the writer might wonder whether or not he was seriously involved with a woman. Lily the woman simply closed that particular door in her mind.

Lily the writer might wonder about his mysterious past. She loved mysterious pasts. She could dream one up at the drop of a hat for any stranger who happened to catch her eye, and Curt Powers positively radiated mystery. Mystery number one being all those scars he made no effort to hide.

Oh, yes, Lily the writer was an expert at reading people. She had learned in a hard school, graduating magna cum whatever. It was Lily the woman who was in trouble. The deeper she delved, the more attracted she was, and she didn't even know what made him tick. She did know that while he might think all his old wounds had healed over, he still had some inner healing to do. She'd seen children who'd been severely beaten, their fragile bones snapped like twigs. Even when the physical injuries healed, the internal scars remained. After all these years she still had scars of her own.

Curt Powers had a few secrets to go along with those scars of his. She would bet her last dollar on that.

"You mentioned a deadline," Curt reminded her on the morning of day six. The sun had barely risen over the dunes. Just back from his morning swim, he'd encountered her on the front porch, egg sandwich in hand, taking advantage of a warm, sluggish breeze.

"I mailed back my contract yesterday. Technically I don't have to start my next book until it's countersigned and returned."

"You're the one who mentioned a deadline. If you need to get back, don't let me stop you." He felt compelled to needle her for no real reason other than the oppressive heat. That and the fact that she was beginning to seriously get under his skin in a way that was damned hard to hide. Especially in swim trunks.

"Look, if you want me to leave, just say so. No, you don't even have to do that. Just help me carry those damned boxes out to my car, and I'll get out of your way!"

It was the heat, he told himself. It was getting to her, too. That and the sexual tension that was never far from the surface. Swearing softly, he raked his fingers through his damp hair. "Sorry. Just trying to make polite conversation."

"Buy an instruction book," she snapped.

"Or quit trying." His rueful smile was a tacit surrender. Point to you, madam.

After the first day, he had gone back to his routine of rising early, working out before the sun got too hot—not that there was much of a differential here on the Outer Banks where the temperature was influenced more by the surrounding waters than by the sun. Then, after he tortured his muscles as much as he dared, he would head for the beach, hit the surf and swim until he could barely drag himself back home.

Next came a shower—first hot, then cold. Then he would dress and get back to those yellowed, crumbling, mostly boring old papers, working wherever she wasn't, trying to focus his mind on exploring his roots instead of exploring what he'd like to be exploring. Namely the woman Lily O'Malley.

Having survived all these years without roots—at least without knowing about his own—he was somewhat surprised to find himself increasingly determined to learn more about the ancestor who had sailed the high seas in an age when nuclear subs were considered science fiction.

When the entire twenty-first century had been science fiction.

If there was a clue in one of those boxes as to the final resting place of the old man's ship, it was either written in code or buried in one of Bess's mawkish novels. He didn't even know why it mattered, but then, he'd always been a sucker for a challenge. It was one of the reasons he'd joined the SEALS.

"Sorry," Lily said quietly. "I'm so hot I can't even breathe. Could we please start over?"

Standing there in his trunks, with a wet towel draped strategically around his hips, he was tempted to tell her what he'd like to start. Instead, he said, "Sure."

"Nice swim?" She forked a finger between the pages of the diary she'd been reading and tried to look as if she cared.

"Not particularly. Water's too warm." It came out as a snarl, so he stretched his lips into a smile that was about as convincing as the towel around his waist.

She'd piled her hair up on top of her head. It was beginning to slide down, tendrils sticking to her damp face and that shallow valley at the back of her neck that was more tempting than the cleavage on any other woman.

Stand down, sailor! He was beginning to breathe hard again. Twenty minutes of body surfing, a jog across a quarter mile of soft sand and his pulse rate hadn't even shifted into second gear. One look at the woman daintily blotting egg yolk from her mouth and he was all messed up again. Could perpetual horniness be a side effect of cutting his medication too fast?

"By the way, did you know you have mice?" she asked.

"So?"

"I just thought I'd mention it, in case you were tempted to leave food out. Mice like paper, too—at least they like to nest in it."

He was tempted, all right, but it had nothing to do with food or mice or paper. He continued to watch for a minute, towering over her while the salt slowly dried on his skin. She went back to her reading—didn't even glance up.

And then she did, giving him that cool look she had down pat—the one he interpreted as *Buzz off, dude, I'm somebody and you're nobody.*

Which more or less summed up his own feelings at the moment. Biggest mistake of his life, bringing her here. He was beginning to regret even coming here himself. Wheeling away, he strode down the hall to his room, slammed the door, leaned against it for a moment, then hobbled across the floor, moving like an old man. Like the thirty-six-year-old washed-up has-been he was. If he'd been here alone he'd have stripped, stretched out on the bed with the fan blowing across him and slept until starvation drove him out to forage for food.

Instead, he shucked out of his damp trunks and pulled on a pair of clean, dry briefs. No point in clogging up his drainpipes with any more sand. Grabbing his last clean pair of khakis, he headed for the office to see what he could do about mouse-proofing a few cardboard boxes. It hadn't occurred to him before, but dammit, he hadn't gone to all this trouble just to provide a convenient nest for a bunch of rodents. Food was replaceable. Those papers weren't.

He could have bought traps or even poison, but for a guy who'd been trained as a professional bad dude—a lethal dude, to be more precise—he was rapidly losing his taste for killing.

So he had a few mice. So he had a few bugs. For all he knew, he might have a few reptiles. The last time it had rained, he'd found three tree frogs on his bedroom wall. But bad dude or not, he didn't feel like engaging in another search and destroy mission, not here in his own territory.

Which meant finding something—maybe the tool chest in the back of his truck—that would serve as a safe until he went through the papers, took out any he wanted to keep, gave Bess's stuff to Lily and turned the rest over to the local museum.

He heard the front screen swing shut. Sensed her presence before she spoke.

Only she didn't speak, so he glanced up and she did that

expressive thing with her eyebrows, which, roughly translated, meant "What the hell are you up to *now?*"

He was getting good at reading her. For a lady who made her living with words, she got a lot of mileage from a few silent, subtle gestures.

"You're right. Might be better to stash these things where they won't get chewed up before we're done with them." He was in a surly mood, a challenging mood. In the mood for a good, clear-the-air fight, only he couldn't come up with any reasonable grounds.

"Good idea. Those old newspaper clippings are crumbling, anyway, but I'd hate to see them turned into mice nests."

No jumping up on a chair and holding her skirts. Not that he'd expected her to. Besides, the lady wore slacks. She had the kind of body that looked great in pants, ditto that silk thing she'd been wearing the first time he'd seen her in person.

The kind that made a man wonder how she would look wearing nothing at all.

"I thought I'd stash 'em in the tool chest in my truck. We can take out a few stacks at a time to work on."

No argument. "I'll help you," she said, and, lifting the smallest of the boxes, she headed out the front door with it. For a woman who didn't strike him as particularly muscular, she had a surprising amount of upper-body strength.

Working together, they emptied the toolbox and stored all six boxes except for the items they were currently working on. For Curt it was the logbooks. Somewhere in one of them, there might even be a clue to the *Black Swan*'s last voyage. So far about all he'd discovered was that the old man had a woman aboard and a kid named Annie, and that between the two of them they had him wrapped around their little fingers, even after Annie threw up all over his best boots. It was all there, between bills of lading and weather data.

Lily kept out all five of Bess's diaries, but none of the novels. He was tempted to tell her to take what she wanted with his blessings. If she planned to stay until she'd read everything the woman had ever written, he would be climbing the walls. He could walk into a room an hour after she'd been there and sense her presence. Seeing her things lined up alongside his in the bathroom, he couldn't even shave without cutting himself.

Hanging over the side of the truck, she held up a bundle of letters tied together with a faded ribbon. "Have you read any of these?"

"Not yet."

"Do you mind if I keep them out? I mean, they're probably personal."

"And the diaries aren't?" he mocked.

She shrugged, and Curt wished he didn't notice the way her shirt slid over her body. There was nothing at all seductive about what she was wearing now, or any of the other outfits she'd worn since she'd been here. They certainly weren't what he'd have expected a famous author to wear. But they had the same effect as if she'd been wearing one of those silky things cut up to here and down to there.

Good thing she stuck to baggy cottons.

Good thing he wasn't up to peak condition.

Good thing neither one of them was up for anything of an intimate nature.

"Help yourself," he growled. Reaching past her, Curt slammed down the lid. Startled, Lily fell back. If he hadn't been standing there—if his arms hadn't closed around her reflexively, she'd have fallen to the ground.

That was all it took. The fuse had been smoldering for days.

Six

The kiss was hungry, hot, devastating. With a sultry sun beating down from a cloudless sky, they held on desperately, hands slipping on sweat-slick flesh, until the first explosive force was expended. Even then, neither of them made an effort to break away. They clung together for support, struggling for breath.

Curt's hands moved over her shoulders, exploring their way down the delicate bones of her back, cupping the swell of her hips to press her against his aching groin. Their mouths joined once again, almost awkward in their eagerness.

Out on the highway, a car whipped past, horn blowing. Dazed, they broke apart, staring as if neither of them could believe what had just happened. Curt knew as surely as he knew his own name that it wasn't going to end here. This thing—whatever it was—had been simmering beneath the surface since the first time he'd seen her in her silk and pearls, with that fake smile and that haughty "back-off" look in her eyes.

And she knew it, too.

Oh, yes, Lily knew it. Knew that no matter how much she wanted to deny the inevitable, she couldn't do it. Eve and that damned apple. The dark, sweet taste of temptation—of his mouth on hers, his hands on her body. Wherever they were headed, she was going willingly, knowing she'd be hurt in the end, because there was no way on earth she could protect herself against something so powerful, so wonderful—so compelling. For the first time in her life she knew what it must be like to be addicted. To need—to want so desperately that nothing else in the world mattered.

It was Curt who finally broke away. His hands left her breasts, moved down her arms, tangled with her fingers for a moment and then…let go.

Lily sagged toward him, desperately needing his arms around her, his strength. Needing him to hold her, at least until the world settled down again, but he shook his head. Gently, almost sadly, he stood his ground. "If you're looking for an apology, forget it."

God knows where it came from—pride, mostly—but Lily found the strength to lift her head and look him coolly in the eyes. "Did I ask for an apology?"

The good news was that he appeared to be almost as shaken as she was.

The bad news was that on his part, it was no more than a temporary physical condition. She knew all about easy sex. Knew who took, who gave and who ended up suffering most. She had no intention of becoming a victim of hit-and-run sex.

"Well, at least we got that out of our systems." Suspecting her act might fall a bit short of the mark, she tilted her chin and held his gaze as long as she dared, then turned toward the house.

It was only a kiss, dammit. It meant about as much as…as ketchup on fries. Nice, but hardly necessary.

She trudged through the sand, climbed the three wooden steps to the front porch, resisting the urge to turn and see if he was watching her. That burning sensation between her shoulder blades was probably only a laser beam from a passing spaceship.

The Lily who lived deep inside her, who never lied to her, whispered that it was a good thing he wasn't all that interested, because if he'd led her to his bed, she wouldn't have uttered a word. Not so much as a weak whimper, to her everlasting shame. It was bad enough that she wanted him so much she ached, without having to prove to herself that she was her mother's daughter.

Neither of them spoke about their mutual lapse in judgment. For the rest of the day they avoided each other, speaking only when necessary.

"We're about out of coffee."

"I'll put it on the list."

"Have you seen my keys?"

"They're by the phone."

She added it to the growing list of flaws. He misplaced things and lacked the patience to look for them. That and his various physical infirmities should have dimmed his appeal. The trouble was that underneath that gruff, imperfect exterior, there was a wounded warrior who was beginning to bring out protective instincts she hadn't even known she possessed.

Unfortunately, those weren't the only instinct he aroused. Aside from wanting to comfort him, to offer to be his friend for life and then curl up in the security of his strong arms, there was this other thing—the explosive sexual attraction. Lily was pretty sure he didn't welcome it any more than she did, but there it was. It was nothing she hadn't described dozens of times in her books, yet ironically, she'd never before experienced it personally.

After spending hours trying to decipher faded, spidery handwriting, Lily gave up. Even when she could make out the words, following the obscure mind trails of a woman who had lived in an earlier century required more concentration than she could bring to the task at the moment.

Laying aside the stack of letters and diaries she'd been comparing, she wandered aimlessly through the empty rooms, absorbing the ambience. It was the way she worked best—gathering impressions, allowing them to sink in, to coalesce into something tangible. If she'd been a painter, she would have been an Impressionist.

After her second book had been published, she had attempted to use one of the countless tried-and-true methods for plotting. For days she had followed the prescribed course, charting conflicts and resolutions, action and reaction. Finally she had given up in defeat and gone back to allowing her subconscious mind to lead the way.

Like the radio interference that was so prevalent here on the island, Curt's presence was everywhere. She did her best to filter him out and focus on Bess. Sometimes it seemed almost as if she were losing her grasp on reality, something she'd been accused of more than once.

There was one room in particular that gave her the oddest feeling of…closeness. Almost as if, with a little effort, she could reach back through the fog of time and touch…

Someone. Something.

She could just imagine Curt's reaction if she were to try to describe it. "You're trying to tell me you see *ghosts?*"

"No, I'm trying to tell you I feel things. Impressions, that's all."

"Sure you do, sweetheart," he'd say. And then he would hum a few bars from that old TV show, meaning she was bonkers. Nothing new about that. Even as a child she used to disappear inside her own head when things got too ugly on the outside. Some had made fun of her—others had tried to take advantage of her. After the first few attempts, they'd quickly learned to leave her alone.

She made two sandwiches since she was making, and took Curt's to the office. This policy of conscious avoidance took too much energy.

He was hunched over an untidy array of charts. Sensing her presence, he glanced over his shoulder, and it struck her all over again that whatever the quality certain men had that drove women out of their mind—machismo or something—he had more of it than the law allowed. Ignoring the stuff was like trying to ignore a tornado, but she gave it her best shot.

"Hi. You forgot to eat." When he didn't immediately chase her out of the room, she ventured further. "Curt, d'you know what I think?"

Reaching for the thick cheese and salsa sandwich, he said a bit warily, "Thanks. I forgot about food. Should I know what you're thinking?"

That garnered a quick grin. "Not really. Just a figure of speech."

He waited. Lily took a big bite and chewed thoughtfully while she assembled her courage. "I've been reading letters from Bess's gentleman friend, Horace. I'm pretty sure he was a lawyer, and as her name ended up being Bagby, she must've married him before she died. Anyway, comparing the dates on the letters with the dates in her diary, I get the feeling she was behind something that happened here between old Matthew and his wife—your great-great-grandmother Rose.''

"My grandmother who?"

"Rose. That was her given name, didn't you know?"

"No, I—actually, I don't know much about my family history. That's one of the reasons why these papers are so important to me.''

Was it her imagination, or was he trying to make her feel guilty all over again for buying the things? She'd thought they'd gotten past that, or at least reached a compromise. "Well, of course they are. I didn't think it was because you were into recycling,'' she said dryly. She thought she saw a flash of laughter in his eyes, but it disappeared too quickly to be sure. He muttered something about a smart mouth, and took a bite of his sandwich.

Emboldened, she moved closer, standing behind him to look over his shoulder. "These aren't old. What are all those?"

"Geodetic surveys. Comparative studies of the shoreline, showing the rate of erosion over the past hundred years.''

"Why?"

"Why what? Erosion? Littoral currents. Storms.''

Curt knew what she meant. Why was he so interested. Not entirely comfortable with the answer, he countered with a question of his own. "Why are you so determined to pry into my family's secrets?''

It took her a moment. He could almost see the wheels spinning, but she was quick. "After a hundred years, I'm not sure you could call them secrets. Isn't there a statute of limitations or something?''

Wildflowers. Yep, that's what it was, all right. He didn't know if she bathed in the stuff or rolled in it—it was subtle, little more than the occasional whiff—but that was enough. "Tell you what—I'll trade my secrets for yours. One for one. Pick your generation and start talking. For instance, where're you from? I can't seem to pin down your accent."

Her jaw fell. She had a nice jaw. More stubborn than it looked. Nice teeth, too, although she could have done with braces when she was younger. "You're not serious."

"Dead serious. Try me."

He waited, enjoying the inner battle. She had secrets, all right. What woman didn't? Trouble was, she was a fiction writer. Like Bess. Lied and made a living at it, only she wouldn't call it lying. Women never did.

Oh, for goodness' sake, Curtis, stop pestering me about your father, he didn't want us, and that's all you need to know!

But why didn't he want us, Mama? Did I do something bad?

If you must know, he got sick and died. Like Badger.

You mean he ate poison meat?

I mean—oh, for goodness' sake, people die, that's all. They just…do!

"Where did you disappear to just then?" Lily asked curiously.

"Where did I what?"

She hooked the stool with her foot, dragged it closer and sat down. "For a minute you looked as if you were a thousand miles away. I feel that way, too, sometimes. Like I just slip back in time to another era, another place. And to answer your question, Boston, Baltimore, Detroit, Norfolk. Mostly."

He frowned down at the geodetic survey. As if they hadn't been walking on eggshells ever since that business out by the truck, she slid the thing closer and pretended to study it. Deliberately he breathed in the scent of her hair, her skin. A hair of the dog, he thought with bitter amusement. Or maybe a vaccination.

For all her inconsistencies, he was beginning to get a sense of Lily the woman, as opposed to Lily the successful writer. The first time he'd seen her, wearing a tailored suit of some rough silk material, with matching shoes and a string of pearls around her throat, he'd barely noticed the fact that she was one fine-looking woman. At the time he'd been stiff and sore, and mad as hell at having to drive all the way to Norfolk to track down a woman who had knowingly walked off with property she knew damned well she wasn't entitled to.

That image had begun to blur. Seeing her here day after day, he was coming to know the woman behind the facade, and that was a different Lily entirely. One who combined guts, class and a sense of humor. One whose vocabulary was better than his, yet who admitted that her education wasn't quite all it should be. A woman who was basically honest, but not above using questionable means to get what she wanted.

A woman who had screwed up his judgment—one who was hiding something besides the stash of junk food he happened to know she carried in that bag of hers. He might not have discovered all the secrets behind those rainwater-clear eyes of hers, but he wasn't finished with her yet.

"Secrets, remember? We're going to trade off, one to one?" she reminded him. "I told you where I was from, so now you owe me."

If there was one trait Curt could lay claim to, it was tenacity. It was what had gotten him through a childhood made miserable by personal doubts, by being the new kid in a small town where new kids were made to prove themselves by taking on every schoolyard bully and beating the stuffing out of them.

Which he had eventually done, much to the disgust of his mother.

It was all that had got him through BUD/s training and everything that had followed. It had carried him through one disastrous, heavy-duty love affair and a few lesser ones. It had got him through a muddy hell in a river with an unpronounceable name in the jungles of Central America.

He had a feeling that same tenacity was about to drag him into more trouble than he'd bargained for. Him and his big mouth.

"I had a dog named Badger when I was five," he said flatly, daring her to make something of it.

Instead, she studied him under a sweep of lashes that ought to be registered and controlled as a lethal substance. Did she do it deliberately? Was she aware than he could see the swell of her small breasts in the open throat of her shirt? Either she was a whole lot smarter or a whole lot more naive than he'd first thought. For the life of him, he couldn't decide.

"Okay, I guess we're even. Here's a freebie. I never had a pet."

"Speaking of secrets, you've had access to six boxes of mine," he reminded her.

"Of Bess's secrets, maybe, but not yours. Besides, hers were published, so that makes them in the public domain."

"Her diaries?"

She shrugged. It was a beautiful thing to see, with the thin cotton of her shirt sliding over her small breasts. "Okay, I'll give you that one. You want secrets about my distant relatives? Sorry. I don't even know the names of my grandparents."

"How can you not know the names of your grandparents?"

"Easy. I was found under a cabbage plant by a stork who had amnesia. There, now it's your turn again." She stood and stretched, and he nearly reached out and clasped a hand around her waist. Came damned close to it, it was that tempting. Seemed that natural. "I think I'll go outside and, um, walk awhile," she said in that tone he was coming to mistrust.

"Yeah, why don't you do that?"

And while you're at it, get old and ugly and cranky, come back bitching and smelling of garlic and sweat. That way we might be able to stick it out a few more days, until one or the other of us throws in the towel.

Determined to concentrate on the task at hand so that Lily could take what papers he didn't want and leave, Curt spent the rest of the day sorting and skimming. Old letters, bills of lading, manifestos and personal memos—"bring home a doll for Annie, a peach tree and a bolt of calico," all scrawled in faded ink, in a now familiar angular script. He was beginning to feel like an intruder. Who was Annie? Where was the peach tree? Why did he even care?

Because the truth was that he was beginning to care. Something no self-respecting rolling stone could afford to do.

Flexing a back that had grown increasingly stiff from hours of sitting in the same position, he anchored the various stacks against an errant breeze with a few clamshells he used for the purpose, and wandered out onto the porch. Lily was dozing over one of Bess's novels. "Want to go swimming?"

She glanced up, blinked several times and said, "What time is it?"

"Nearly eight. Still plenty of light left, though. We can

order pizzas, take a dip and be back by the time they're delivered.''

Bad idea. Lousy idea, but then, he was full of those. Bringing Lily here rated right up there at the top of the list of bad ideas.

"You're kidding, right? Secret number whatever is that I can't swim.''

"So fake it.''

"Curt, I don't own a bathing suit, and even if I did, I'm not about to walk across miles of blistering hot sand just to get wet. That's what showers are for.''

"The sand's cooled off, and salt's good for your skin.''

"There's nothing wrong with my skin.''

He wouldn't touch that one with a ten-foot oar. "Come on, you need a break.''

In the stare-down contest, Curt won, hands down. They met a few minutes later on the front porch. Lily was wearing a pair of baggy shorts that came almost to her knees, with the same men's shirt she'd worn all day now knotted at her waist.

"This'll have to do,'' she said defiantly.

Remembering the woman he'd first seen behind a tableful of books, wearing a classy silk outfit with a string of pearls around her throat, Curt could only nod. It would do. Oh, hell yeah, it would do just fine.

They set out across the stretch of sandy yard. Behind them the calm waters of the Pamlico mirrored a faithful reflection of a pink-and-gold sky that shaded off into colors he couldn't begin to describe. Before them, each stunted, wind-sculpted yaupon and cedar cast a lavender shadow on the peach-colored sand.

Staring entranced at the sky, Lily stumbled. He caught her, but quickly released her. And then, fool that he was, standing near the edge of the narrow highway that ran the length of the island, he reached for her hand again. Fingers entwined, they waited until traffic passed. Cars with surfboards or kayaks on top, SUVs with bumper racks of fishing gear. Once it was clear, they crossed the soft, warm asphalt to the other side. "Rush-hour traffic, I've been told, lasts roughly from early June through Labor Day."

Lily smiled and made an effort to ease her hand from his, but when he held on, she didn't make an issue of it. Maybe he needed the support, although she didn't think so. He was moving much easier these past few days, as though he was no longer afraid of stepping on a land mine. It had been the first thing Lily had noticed about him—the way he moved. Like a jungle animal, she remembered thinking at the time. Even then she'd sensed a certain predatory element in the man.

Nothing had happened since to change her mind.

She had to hurry to keep up with his long-legged stride. "You doing okay?" he asked, and she nodded breathlessly. She happened to know he worked out in his room every morning before jogging across to the beach for his swim. An hour later he would come back, sweat dripping from every pore, trying to pretend he wasn't exhausted, that he wasn't ready to drop in his tracks. She'd asked him once if he was sure he should be exerting himself in his condition, and he'd snapped something to the effect that yeah, he should, and his condition was none of her business, so butt out.

She was trying to butt out, but it wasn't easy. "Know what? I really miss sidewalks," she panted.

"Plenty of sidewalks in Norfolk."

In other words, she interpreted, get off my island. Ignoring the unsubtle hint and the surprising way it hurt, she said, "My shoes are full of sand."

"Take 'em off."

"What, and blister my feet?"

"Sand's not all that hot," he dismissed.

"Not if you're used to it, maybe." He obviously was. The soles of his feet must be tough as leather, for all they were nice feet. Long and narrow, high-arched, with a dusting of dark hair on the top.

Oh, for Pete's sake, now she was getting turned on by a man's feet! There was a name for that sort of kinkiness. "Sure, and spend the rest of the night picking cactus needles out of my toes," she muttered.

They were still holding hands. She made it, puffing and panting, to the crest of the dunes, then stood and gazed out over the glittery surface of the ocean in awe. Every ripple on a cobalt surface was rimmed with gold. A lazy curl of pink foam edged each wave where it brushed the shore. "Oh, my," she whispered.

"You can do better than that. You're a writer."

"Some things are best left to the imagination."

He took her hand again while she shed her shoes, one after the other, and tossed them back up on the dry sand. Then he led her down to the water's edge, where a shallow, lace-edged wave curled about their ankles.

"See the moon?" Following his pointing finger, she saw the pale crescent directly overhead. "Means the tide's dead low. Good time for your first swimming lesson."

"Whoa. I'm still not sure this is a good idea. I mean, doesn't it take some, uh—conditioning?"

"Can you float?"

"How the devil do I know? My bathtub's too short to try it."

Curt opened his mouth to comment, thought better of it and took a firmer grip on her hand. With no wind and the tide all the way out, there was no more than a slight surface chop. Personally, he preferred an incoming tide with a moderate current, even a bit of undertow to pit his strength against, but if she'd never even been in a swimming pool, this was as good as it got.

Ankle deep, and she was hanging on to his hand like a life preserver. The sandy bottom was hard, no sloughs or gullies. They waded out until the water lapped at the hem of her shorts, and she turned and beamed up at him like a kid who'd just kicked his training wheels.

"This is nice," she said in that breathy, husky voice she used when she was excited over some new discovery in one of Bess's diaries. "I sort of thought it would be colder."

Ignoring her words, he watched her face. What he saw there threw him into another tailspin. "Who the devil are you?" he asked softly.

"What? I don't understand."

She looked every bit as confused as he was beginning to feel, but he wasn't about to let her off the hook. "You claim to be Lily O'Malley—"

"I am Lily O'Malley!" She shook her hand free from his, then clutched his arms as another wave swept up past her waist. The tide was beginning to turn.

"Right. You're Lily O'Malley, famous writer. Newspaper reporters recognize you, people line up for your autograph. You wear genuine pearls and hoard food, even wrapping leftover slices of pizza—" He cut off her automatic protest. "Oh, yeah, I've seen that pack you carry like you're not sure where your next meal's coming from."

"You searched my personal property?" She looked so distressed he wished he could unsay that last. Sure he'd checked out what she called her personal property. He figured she owed him that much under the circumstances. Besides, he hadn't trusted her as far as he could see her those first few days. If she was packing, he damn well needed to know it.

No gun. Candy bars, cookies, peanuts—every kind of junk food available, plus some floppy disks and the usual female stuff. One of those miniature purses women seemed to like, a lipstick, keys, wads of tissue and three pens. "Nah, I didn't actually search it," he lied, ashamed of himself even though all he'd done was assure himself that she wouldn't catch him off guard and do God knows what. "But, yeah, I checked you out. I'd be a fool not to."

"Like I was a fool to go home with you, you mean?" She looked so hurt he was ready to forgive her everything, stealing his personal property—forcing him into doing something he'd had no intention of doing.

"Damn right you were. What if I'd been a rapist? A murderer? What if I'd held you for ransom?"

"Like somebody would actually pay ransom for me?" she scoffed, trying unconvincingly to sound as if she couldn't care less.

"Your publisher?"

It took a minute to sink in. Slowly she nodded. She was still hanging on to his arm. The tide was still washing around them—not yet a problem, but incoming, all the same.

"Hey, lighten up and let's go. We're wasting time, and the tide's starting to change," he said, his voice dangerously close to tender.

"I don't like for people to intrude on my privacy."

"Duly noted. Matter of fact, neither do I," he said with significant emphasis. "However, we seem to be stuck with each other for the time being, so why not declare a truce and make the best of it? Deal?"

While he waited for her to make up her mind, he felt the sand shift under his feet as the current grew stronger.

No matter how benign things looked on the surface, he knew better than to underestimate any situation. "You don't want to waste a great opportunity, do you? Never know when you'll find yourself in over your head."

"Again," she said drolly.

"Again," he echoed, offering what he hoped was a reassuring smile.

"Well...I guess. But I'm not ready to swim yet. Maybe we could start with floating?"

"You got it, but first, let's get out past these breakers."

He led her out past the bar, to where the swells were just starting to make up. Standing shoulder deep—her shoulders, not his—he waited until she got the feel of the gentle currents before issuing instructions. Somewhat to his surprise, she trusted him enough to lie back on his arm, allowing him to support her while she floundered for balance.

"Easy, just let go. You're stiff as a crowbar. Let your arms and legs relax...that's it. I'll keep your head above water, you don't have to—yeah, that's great. You're a natural."

"Look, Ma—it's me, Lily. I'm floating on top of the ocean." She laughed aloud. He felt something shift deep inside him that had nothing to do with incoming tides or littoral currents.

A few moments later he eased his arm away, but brought it back under her shoulders when her face went under. "You let me go," she accused, gasping, sputtering, blinking reddening eyes. He was still holding her, but the trust was broken. She grabbed him around the waist, hooked one hand into the waistband of his trunks and said, "I can't do this! You're trying to drown me!"

"You know better than that. Come on now, a few minutes more and we'll call it a day." The seas were forcing her against him, and there was nothing either of them could do about it. A few more minutes with her hanging on to his pants and he'd never make it to shore—at least not without embarrassing himself. The water was tepid. What he needed right now was an ice-cold shower.

Firmly he removed her fingers, held her at arm's length and carefully positioned her to try again. "Come on, Lily, one more time and then we'll call it quits. This time, let's do it right. Up you go—I've got you, I'll hold your head, all you have to do is concentrate on relaxing. Easy, easy, I've still got you."

She did it because he was bigger than she was. Because she was way out of her depth and they both knew it. He'd have to hand it to her—she didn't panic. Just one more facet of Lady Lily. For a civilian she was pretty damn cool under fire.

After a few minutes Curt eased her into an upright position. He waited until she was steady on her feet, then stepped back, still holding her arm because the tide was rising fast. "You did great. Tomorrow you'll be ready for the next step."

"Any step I take tomorrow will carry me as far as the front porch, and that's it. As long as I stay away from boats and floodplains in the future, chances are I probably won't drown."

"What about bathtubs? You ever hear of home accidents?"

"So I'll hose off outside," she said, but that husky note of laughter was back in her voice.

"How come you never learned to swim?" he asked as they waded ashore.

"What, another secret? I think you owe me." Lily had refused to hold his hand once she was sure she could walk without having a wave catch her in the back and tumble her head over heels. Now that her lesson was over, she was almost sorry she'd given up so soon. Not that she'd expected to actually learn to swim her first time in the ocean. Like all her other attempts at making up for past educational gaps, she was good at going after exactly what she needed at the moment, faking the rest and writing around any hazardous roadblocks.

Still, it would've been nice, for once, to succeed her first time out. *Look, Ma, no hands! That was me, Lily, out there floating on top of the ocean!*

"I don't know," she said with a careless shrug. "I just never got around to it."

How many times had she begged to be taken to the beach, or even to the pool at the community center? How many times had her mother put her off with some excuse or another? They couldn't afford it. She was expecting company. She had a headache.

And that was in the early days, when she'd still bothered to make excuses.

"Tomorrow we'll start teaching you to swim."

"You don't know when to quit, do you? Look, Curt, I appreciate it, I really do, but for the short time I'll be here, it's hardly worth the effort."

The sky was still a blaze of color, but the first few stars were beginning to show. "Jupiter," he said, pointing to a bright point of light out over the ocean.

She nodded and tried to swallow past the lump in her throat. Here she was, in a picture-postcard-perfect moment, and all she felt was sadness. Why couldn't they have been an ordinary couple on vacation instead of who they were? Strangers—a man who had accused a woman of stealing his property, and the woman who refused to give it back.

Bess, are you watching? Are you listening? Are you getting a big laugh out of this mess you landed me in?

Seven

Sometime before morning Curt opened his eyes in the darkness and lay perfectly still, all senses instantly alert. Something—someone—had roused him from a vivid dream of jungle vines, twisting and twining around his body, pulling him under. He'd been struggling to escape when a bank of flowers had detached from the shore and drifted toward him, surrounding him, buoying him up, dizzying him with their heavy fragrance.

Shaking off the dream, he listened, hearing only the sound of thunder in the distance. A passing vehicle. The drone of a mosquito somewhere in the room. Normal sounds. Nothing to set his heart to pounding—until every beat sent blood rushing through his arteries, like the sound of heavy footsteps in gravel.

Carefully he eased out of bed and stood, waiting to get his bearings. Nothing hurt, thank God. If he had to go one on one, he was pretty sure he could handle it, but he'd rather not put it to the test.

Quietly he opened the locker at the foot of his bed and lifted out a 9 mm SIG-Sauer. Not that he expected to need it—it was probably only Lily, nosing through those old diaries again. She was obsessing on Bess, and he was obsessing on sex. Of the two, hers was the safer choice. That swimming lesson had come a little too close to blowing his circuits.

His back flat against the wall, he waited until his eyes had adjusted to the darkness, then eased toward her room. Her door was open. She hadn't put up an argument when he'd explained that cross ventilation didn't work if doors were closed. No need to mention that he was borderline claustrophobic.

Attuned to the slightest sound, he listened to her slow, even breathing. Clouds had covered the moon, but he didn't need to see her to know that her hair would be spread, a dark tangle on the pillow, and that she would be sleeping on her stomach with one arm dangling off the bed, the other fist against her chin. He had pictured her that way too many times. Imagined himself waking her from a bad dream, offering comfort....

It hadn't been Lily he'd heard. Which meant that someone—or something—had been messing around his house. Whatever it was, it was gone now. At least that itchy feeling was gone. His body might have taken a beating, but there was nothing wrong with his senses, and at the moment they were registering only the familiar grit of sand under his bare feet, the damp chill of night air on his body and the presence of another body in the vicinity.

Lily. Even sleeping, she was a big blip on his radar screen.

But because he was awake and still keyed up, he quietly

let himself outside and checked out the area. Screens all secure, both outside doors locked. There were enough empty cottages, even early in September, so that a house that was obviously inhabited wouldn't be particularly attractive to someone looking for an easy mark. Prime targets were surfboards and fishing gear left underneath cottages or inside vehicles.

Probably a raccoon, he concluded, laying the 9 mm on a kitchen counter while he removed the milk carton from the refrigerator. No point in going back to bed, it would soon be morning.

The air was almost cool for a change. Judging from the frequent flashes of lightning out over the ocean, any possibility of rain had passed them by. Still, he liked the predawn hours. Best time in the world for sorting things out in his mind, and God knows, he had plenty to sort through. The list grew longer each day. Whether or not to make his retirement official. And if he did, what kind of job to look for. He knew demolition. He knew men. Thanks to the Navy, he had a degree, and the job market was wide open. Money was no problem. He'd invested well, relying on hunches rather than expert advice. Holed up here on the island he could live modestly well on interest and dividends until he decided on his next move.

Lily was a problem. The one thing he hadn't figured on was a woman.

Thank God she was strictly temporary.

Leaving his gun behind, he moved outside, lowered himself stiffly onto the front porch rocker, savoring the cool dampness on his almost-bare backside. He'd taken the time to pull on a pair of briefs, but that was all. He was still there a few minutes later, watching lightning flicker out over the ocean, when he sensed a presence behind him.

"Am I intruding?" Lily asked softly.

"Yeah, you are, not that that'll stop you."

"You know me pretty well."

"Better than I want to." But not as well as he'd like to in a strictly carnal sense.

She was wearing a pair of men's pajamas, long-legged, long-sleeved, buttoned up to her chin. How the devil could a woman look seductive in a pair of striped pj's? "Might as well pull up a chair," he growled softly. The two porch chairs were close enough that he could smell the sleep on her. There was no perfume in all the world as arousing as the scent of a woman still warm from her bed.

"I saw your gun in the kitchen," she remarked casually.

"So?" As a conversational gambit, that one was going nowhere.

"Are you a cop?"

"Do I look like a cop?"

"You look like a man with a bad back, some nasty scars—a man who wears black drawers and has the sweet disposition of a junkyard dog."

"I'd say that about covers it."

Neither of them spoke for the next few minutes. Curt could have kicked himself for leaving his gun out in plain sight. He knew better than that.

"Going somewhere?" He was staring pointedly at the car keys fisted in her hand.

"I thought I heard something."

"Thunder."

"I know what thunder sounds like. It's not sneaky."

"*Sneaky?*"

"Like someone trying to break in."

In the lavender, predawn light, he studied her profile. How could a woman be beautiful without being pretty? Was it because Hollywood defined prettiness? "So you were going to tackle some hothead with a set of car keys?"

"I don't own a gun. As you discovered when you searched my tote bag."

She still hadn't forgiven him for that. He couldn't much blame her. "Tell me something—how many of those ladies' self-defense courses have you taken?"

"None of your—three. And you don't have to sound so damned condescending, they're good courses. And by the way," she added smugly, "that's one more secret you owe me."

"Did it ever occur to you that an armed thug doesn't care if you have a pink-plaid belt in chop suey, he's got the edge because he doesn't give a damn if he kills you or not?"

During the thirty seconds of silence that followed, he wanted to believe she was taking his words seriously. "Think about it, Lily. The bad guys don't play by your rules."

"Do you think I don't know that? Believe me, I know how to fight dirty. I know enough to run and hide if there's a chance of running or hiding, but when there's not, I'll use whatever I can lay my hands on as a weapon. You'd be amazed how much damage you can do with a can of roach spray."

"I doubt if roach spray would stop even a rabid raccoon before he inflicted some serious damage."

"Is that what you think it was? The noise that woke me up?"

He thought about lying to her. Decided to try evasion, instead. "What you heard was me checking the windows. When I heard the thunder I wanted to be sure it hadn't rained in before I woke up."

Calm as anything, she uttered a word not usually heard in polite circles. "I heard you prowling around out there, but before that, someone was messing around, testing the screens. If you hadn't got up when you did, he'd have cut one and come inside.''

Pale-gold sunlight limned a three-quarter cameo of her face as he stared at her. "You were asleep."

"I was playing possum. I knew whatever it was, you'd take care of it. That is, if your back didn't freeze up on you. Wanna go look for footprints, now that it's light enough not to trample the evidence? Or have you already stomped all over it?"

He held up a hand while his mind raced to catch up. "Whoa, wait a minute. First you say you were awake when I went into your bedroom, then you say—"

"You didn't come inside, you just stood at the door and listened. I'm good, aren't I? At breath control? I knew this guy who was studying opera, but he got killed in a drive-by."

Slowly Curt shook his head. "Just who the hell are you, Lily O'Malley?" he asked softly. Then, indignantly, he demanded, "And what the hell do you mean, if my back didn't freeze up on me?"

"Sorry. I didn't mean to hurt your pride, but let's face it, you could have needed some help if things had turned out differently. I was ready, you know. If there'd been trouble, I'd have been right there beside you."

"Will you just listen to yourself? God, I can't believe…" He shut his eyes and then opened them again. "Look, bad back notwithstanding, I think I could have handled some punk kid." He scowled, setting the rocker into agitated motion. "Aren't you about finished up here? You've probably got stuff to do back in Norfolk, so don't let me keep you. In fact, if you want to take Bess's books, you're welcome to the lot. Something called *The Virgin and the Vengeful Groom* rates pretty far down on my reading list."

"You're too generous." Her smile was about as sincere as a politician's promise. Roughly translated it meant, Up yours, buster.

"Yeah, I am." His own grim smile wasn't much better. It said, Bug off, lady, before I do something we'll both regret. He knew for a fact that it wasn't necessary to like a woman, or even to know her as a person, to get all hot and bothered. If that had been the case, the X-rated industries would collapse overnight. Besides which, any man who thought he knew a woman deserved what he got. Which was usually the shaft.

Against the background drone of mosquitoes seeking warm blood and the thump of rockers on a sandy, uneven porch floor, they sparred silently. Tested for weaknesses. Curt figured it was pretty much a draw. In spite of his needling, Lily sat there looking as calm as that painting by whatsisname—the *Mona Lisa*. No man with half a brain would turn his back on either of that pair—Mona or Lily.

"What do you think they were after?"

"Raccoons? Garbage, probably."

"It wasn't an animal, and you know it."

"Look, any house this isolated occasionally gets hit. Fact is, it was pretty well cleaned out before I even moved in. Anything of value that could be lugged off was gone by the time I came on the scene. I bought a new mattress, but that's it."

"It's sort of nice, though. Uncluttered, the way a beach cottage should look. I like it the way it is."

He barked a laugh. "What, no rugs, no curtains and damn little furniture?"

"Bare wood has a certain charm, even when it's worn down to the grain. And too much furniture can be…well, too much." She yawned.

"Go to bed," he ordered gruffly.

"I couldn't sleep, even if I did. If I were home, I'd go to work."

"So go to work." He wanted to say, Go home, lady. Get the hell back where you came from and leave me alone, but somewhere in his gene pool there must have been a few decent genes. Just his luck they would kick in when he neither needed nor wanted them.

"Know what I wish? I keep wishing I could get inside Bess's head. She has so many stories to tell, Curt, I just know she does. It sounds crazy, but I keep thinking I was brought here for a purpose. Do you believe in..." She sighed, and he could picture her shoulders lifting and falling, the thin striped cotton of her pajamas sliding over her breasts. "No, of course you don't. Neither do I, not really."

"Glad we cleared that up." There was a hint of amusement in his voice. Just a hint. Not even to himself was he willing to admit how *right* it felt to share the dawn with her, even under these circumstances. To sit here and talk, or not talk, and watch the sky turn pale as shafts of gold heralded the approach of another day.

Reluctantly he rose and headed down the steps. After half a beat, she followed. "Are we looking for evidence?"

"We're looking for whatever's out here. If we're lucky whatever it is will have four feet."

"Or hooves. It could've been a deer. I found deer tracks out near the cemetery the other day."

Neither of them expected to find animal tracks. They found what they were expecting. Footprints. Lug soles, a couple of sizes smaller than his, a couple of sizes larger than hers.

"Now what?" she asked. With the sun behind her, her hair looked like a dark halo. She had rolled her pajama legs up to keep them from trailing through the dew-damp sand. She should have looked absurd. Instead, she looked sexy as hell and about fifteen years old.

"Now nothing. If he comes back tonight, I'll be ready."

"Shouldn't we call the law or something?"

"And report what—footprints?"

"I reported my stalker," she said self-righteously.

"There was no forced entry here, either. No fancy panties tucked in with my briefs. Nothing was taken, and as for trespassing, the place is not posted. Both our vehicles are still there, and I don't have a surfboard or any fishing tackle to steal. If he'd been after a car, he could've hotwired either one of 'em. He didn't. I doubt if he'll be back."

Curt wasn't quite as sanguine as he tried to appear. All it would take was one boozed-up beach bum to create a situation. When and if it happened he'd just as soon not have the responsibility of bodyguarding a celebrity author.

She looked as if she might argue for a minute, but all she said was, "Is there any of that raisin-nut cereal left, do you think?"

After showering and dressing, they met in the kitchen for breakfast. It was still only a few minutes past six, but there was no point in trying to sleep. Finding ants in the cereal, Lily nibbled on a slice of peanut-buttered bread and told Curt to make a list of whatever else he needed. "I'll drive down to the supermarket. I'd like to get away for a little while to sort of put this thing in perspective. Take notes, you know, while it's still fresh in my mind? You might as well know that sooner or later I use just about everything that happens in my books."

"Even swimming lessons?"

She wrinkled her nose. "What about this scenario—bad

guy tries to drown heroine so he won't have to share secret papers with her?''

''Way too obvious. And for your information, I don't *have* to share anything.''

''No? What do you bet the law would side with me? You forfeited your rights when you skipped out on your rent payments.''

''When I *what?* Woman, you are unbelievable. Did anyone ever call you pigheaded?''

''Sure. I took it as a compliment.''

He started to walk away, changed his mind and turned back. He wasn't about to let her have the last word. ''Maybe we both need a change of scenery,'' he growled.

''Fine. I'll wait in the car.''

''Wait in the truck, I'm driving.''

''How about we both drive?'' she countered.

''Lily, don't push me, I'm mean when I don't get enough sleep.''

''Oh? What about the other times? What's your excuse then?'' She was all round-eyed innocence.

''You don't want to know.''

''Mean, chauvinistic, stubborn, suspicious—have I left anything out?''

''Check my personnel file, it's all there.''

''Uh-huh.'' Lily was on to him now. He might not admit it, but he was beginning to like her. Considering the way he could manipulate her feelings, it was a good thing. She'd come a long way, reinventing herself again and again. She wasn't about to back down now on account of a pair of navy-blue eyes and a crooked smile so rare it was on the endangered list.

She was leaning against the warm metal side of the truck, studying the bleak old house, picturing it surrounded by lush shrubbery, when he came outside and locked the door behind him. "I don't need you to go with me, you know," she felt compelled to say. "I'm okay with what happened. It's no big deal."

He sauntered across to where she was standing. "Did I imply otherwise?" he drawled.

"You don't have to. You're mean and suspicious, and your housekeeping is even worse than mine, but evidently you have this protective streak. I just want you to know that I don't need a caretaker."

"Honey, if I decide to take care of you, you'll know it."

The words hung there between them, laden with meaning that neither of them dared explore. She didn't think it had been a deliberate double entendre, but she couldn't be sure.

They drove south in silence. Just north of Little Kinnakeet Lifesaving Station, Curt shoved in a tape. Country western. She should have guessed what type of music he'd like. It could've been worse. A lot worse, she thought, remembering the kind of vicious, heavy metal that used to pummel her for hours at a time while her mother and her friends partied in the next room.

In the supermarket parking lot, Lily pulled a cart from one of the outdoor stands and wheeled it inside. Curt took over, and she let him get away with it. He might think she didn't know when he was hurting, but she wasn't blind. When he was in pain he got a squinty-eyed look, walking in that odd, gliding way that always made her think of dancers and slinking jungle animals.

"Apples, aspirin, ace bandages."

"You and your alphabet," she jeered, wanting to tell him to go outside and wait in the truck, that she'd get whatever they needed. She was just as tough as he was, and she had her own protective streak.

The man had to be crazy, the way he jogged across the hot sand to the beach every morning. Showing off, no doubt. Proving what a macho hero he was. He probably collapsed in agony the minute he reached his bed. "Okay, you do the cart, I'll do the picking. Better yet, go sit in the truck and I'll get what we need and join you in a few minutes. Shall I get ice cream?"

"You want ice cream, get it."

"I only meant are we going to go anywhere else or are we headed directly home?"

"Your choice. You want to procrastinate, why don't we leave the shopping until we're headed north again?"

"I'm not procrastinating, I only thought we could both do with a break."

It occurred to Lily that she'd called it "home." He hadn't caught her up on it. All the same, she wouldn't do it again, because it had sounded too good. And she'd learned the hard way to be wary of anything that sounded too good. Powers Point was his home, not hers. Just because she'd bought some old papers at auction—just because she happened to feel a certain affinity for one of his distant relatives, that didn't mean she had a stake in any part of his life. He had accepted her presence for the time being, but that didn't mean he trusted her.

They drove all the way down through Hatteras village to the ferry docks, stopping for sandwiches and drinks along the way. "Truce?" she asked.

"Truce," he agreed grudgingly. And then he flashed that grin that knocked the wind right out of her sails, as Bess might've said.

They climbed the dunes, sank down on the warm sand and ate in silence, watching a fisherman and a lone surfer. Afterward she tucked the wrappers, napkins and cups into the bag and lay back. "If I fall asleep, wake me before the tide comes in, will you?"

"Don't count on it, I'll be sleeping with you."

When she twisted her head around to gape at him, he laughed softly. "I only meant we both missed some sleep last night."

"Oh." She let it drop, but after a minute, said drowsily, "Isn't it funny how far away everything seems. Like everything that's happened, happened to somebody else?"

"Hmm?" he murmured without opening his eyes.

"Like, you know—trying to drown me yesterday because you hate having to share your family secrets. Like last night—that creep prowling around outside. Like back at my place in Norfolk—and contracts and proposals and agents and publicists, and wondering if I'll make the best-seller lists, and if so, which ones, and how high and how long—and reviews. Out here, it all sort of…fades away."

Her voice trailed off, and Curt allowed the words to settle in his mind. "Navy," he said. "Currently on rehab, considering retirement. How's that for sharing secrets? Now we're even."

Lily rolled over and faced him, her head resting on her arm. "Thank you. It figures—the Navy part, not the retirement." They both fell silent, and then she said, "Sooner or later we probably have to go back to the real world, I guess. At least back to where they have food and bathrooms."

"Did Peter Pan worry about that sort of thing?"

She shrugged. "Beats me. I never met the guy, myself."

"You never read Peter Pan? Lily O'Malley, the most famous author in the Western Hemisphere?"

"Yes, well…as it happens, I know a lot of stuff most people never thought about. I know about people, for instance, and that's mostly what I write about." Lily tried to read his eyes, to tell what he was thinking, but they were narrowed against the glaring sun.

"You know, you could walk away from the heavy stuff if you really wanted to. Simplify your life," he said softly.

"You mean I could turn into a beach bum? Is that what you did?"

After a moment he nodded. "Yeah, I guess it is," he said thoughtfully, his smile catching the glint of the sun. White teeth, laughing eyes in a face that was neither young nor old, but definitely used.

Lily sat up, embraced her knees and gazed out over the Atlantic, thinking of how it had felt for those few moments to float over the surface. Was it possible to drown on dry land? It might explain this feeling of tight-chested breathlessness.

With no more than a slight grimace, Curt got to his feet and held out a hand. "You ready to ride?"

"Ready," she said reluctantly. His eyes were the color of the ocean, way out past the breakers. *Oh, yes, it would be all too easy to drown on dry land.*

They were somewhere between the villages of Frisco and Buxton, in the forested section of the island, when a doe and fawn dashed across the highway in front of the truck. Curt slammed on the brakes and swore. Lily caught her breath and stared.

"Sorry," he said shortly as the pair paused to look back over their upraised tails before dashing into the undergrowth.

"Oh, look," Lily whispered. "It's only a baby...so beautiful..." The deer disappeared, and Lily stared after them, a look of wonder in her eyes. Not until a truck passed illegally on the right hand side of the narrow highway did Curt remember to take his foot off the brake.

"Yeah, well...I never cared much for venison, myself."

She whacked him on the thigh, which made him mutter another apology. It was these crazy feelings that were beginning to pile up inside him. Feelings he didn't understand and sure as hell didn't need. The urge to get under her skin. The urge to apologize.

Instead of heading directly north again, he turned off onto the lighthouse road. "Thought you might as well see her in her new home before you leave."

Before she left. It suddenly struck him that the thought of Lily's leaving didn't seem quite as welcome as it had only a few days ago. Already regretting the impulse, he pulled into a parking space, left the engine running and waited. "If you'd rather not—"

"By her, I take it you mean the lighthouse."

"Yeah. If you're interested. Some people are, some aren't."

"Was this one here when old Matthew was sailing his *Black Swan?*"

"Yeah, I guess. That is, it was moved a few years ago, but comparing the charts, I'd say it probably stood in approximately the same relative position to the shore back in old Matt's day." They got out, walked closer and stared up at the silent sentinel.

His great-great-grandfather had gazed on this same lighthouse. Curt couldn't help but wonder what the old man had thought when he'd seen those spiral stripes after weeks or even months at sea. Relief? A sense of homecoming? Nothing?

Curt tried and failed to clamp the lid down on all the new and unsettling feelings that stirred inside him. It was with a great deal of surprise that he realized a few minutes later that Lily was holding his hand.

Or he was holding hers. "Come on, we'd better get on up the beach."

Back home. Back to Powers Point. Back to the same house where old Matthew had first met Rose, if those damned diaries of Bess's could be believed.

They turned away, Curt striding off in front. Lily took one last look over her shoulder at the towering structure and smiled. He'd rather eat a raw cockroach than admit it, but he was sentimental. *He's coming along nicely, Bess. Blood will tell.*

Eight

By the time they pulled into the driveway, the late-afternoon sun had painted the old house with a flattering glow. Curt had tried not to think of it as home—he wasn't the settling kind—but it was home, all right. It was even beginning to look like a home. Lily had dragged a wooden box, one of the old-style fish boxes, from off the back stoop and set it between the two porch chairs to hold her iced tea and whatever books she was reading. He hadn't noticed when they'd left, but she had set a jar of flowers on it. Those red and yellow things that bloomed all over the beach.

Hell of a note. He might keep the box after she left—it was handy when he wanted to eat or read on the porch, but the flowers would have to go. Next, she'd be wanting to hang curtains and put rugs on his floors.

"I'll bring in the supplies, you put 'em away," he said.

"Is that an order or a suggestion? Because I don't take orders very well."

"I'd noticed," he said, unable to squelch the grin tugging at the corner of his mouth.

"Actually, it's one of my more endearing qualities." She sparked right back at him, and he shook his head and turned back to the truck for another sack of supplies.

Together they put away the groceries and Lily headed out the back door to take in the linens she'd washed and hung the day before. Neither of them was particularly efficient when it came to household tasks. It wasn't until Curt left the kitchen and turned toward his room that the nerves at the back of his neck came alive.

Lily, her arms piled high with sun-dried laundry, was on her way to the bedroom to dump, sort and fold when she nearly slammed into his back. "What's wrong? Curt, what...?" Her voice trailed off as she peered past his shoulder at the office door. It was a paneled door, like all the others, the unpainted wood aged to a rich, dark brown.

"Did you close it?" he asked so softly she had to strain to hear him.

"The door? Of course not. Maybe the wind blew it shut."

"What wind?"

"Right," she echoed, wide-eyed. "What wind?"

He reached for the brown china knob, and she caught his arm. "Fingerprints," she whispered.

"We're not exactly talking high crimes and misdemeanors here," he reminded her. All the same, he used a thumb and forefinger to turn the knob, then nudged the door open with his knee.

"My laptop," she said. When she went to move past him, her arms still full of laundry, he held her back. "But I need to—"

"Wait here. I'll check it out and then see about the rest of the house." It took only a glance to determine that nothing had been touched in the office. His PC and her laptop were side by side on the makeshift desk. And while he couldn't claim a photographic memory, he was pretty sure nothing in the room had been disturbed.

Which was odd… Used computers were a drug on the market, but the information on the hard drives could be of interest to someone who knew how to use it.

He backed out and nodded toward his bedroom. The door was open. At first glance, the room looked pretty much as he'd left it. A shirt on the back of the chair, shoes under the bed—along with a few rolls of lint that stirred as they moved closer.

Lily was two steps behind him. "Where's your gun?"

"You can stop whispering now. Whoever was here is long gone."

"How do you know?"

He gave her a telling look. What was he supposed to say—because the back of his neck was no longer itching? Oh, yeah, that would reassure her all right. "Call it a hunch." It was as close as he would come to admitting to the extrasensory perception that was part training, part experience and part instinct.

"Okay, then where's your gun?"

"Right where I left it, on the closet shelf behind all the junk I had to shift to make room for my diving gear when we converted the toolbox to a mouse-proof storage for all those damned papers."

"Great. You do know that's the first place a thief would search, don't you? A closet shelf." She flung down the stack of linens onto his neatly spread bed. Dust balls scattered. Lily sneezed and said, "You need a housekeeper.

Doris, my housekeeper, would have a fit if she saw all this house moss."

Curt wasn't listening. Dust was the last of his worries. The closet door was one of the few he kept closed—there was no lock, just a hook and eye. It was unhooked. With a sense of growing disquiet, he crossed the room and eased the door open with his left foot.

"What is it? What's wrong? Oh, God, don't tell me— they stole your gun." She was right behind him, peering past his shoulder into the cluttered closet.

It was all there. Apparently nothing was missing. His shirts were still there, stacked on the shelf, rather than hanging. His dress uniforms still in the bags from the cleaners. Two pairs of dress shoes collecting dust, his uniform hat and the duck-bill cap he'd worn before his hair had grown back.

"I see it. I was afraid..." Lily breathed.

"Yeah, me, too."

But he'd been more afraid to find his diving gear missing. Not that he'd be needing the stuff anymore—his diving days were over. But his custom-made dry suit, his tanks, regulators and the rest of his gear—those were a part of who he was. Or rather, who he had been.

"What is it, Curt? What's missing?"

"Nothing."

And that was what was bothering him. Because any thief with half a brain would have cleaned out the dive gear, the gun and both computers. Which left...

"Have you looked in your room? Did you bring any jewelry?"

"Of course I didn't bring any jewelry. My watch..." She held out her wrist, her cuff turned back to reveal an expanse of lightly tanned forearm sporting a small, plain women's wristwatch. It could've been a drugstore quartz—

it could have been one of those five-thousand-dollar jobs. He wouldn't have known the difference.

"Your pearls?"

"In my safe back in Norfolk. Don't worry, I never leave anything lying around."

He pictured her cluttered apartment, every available surface stacked high with books and potted plants. "Right," he said absently, his mind still chewing on the problem of why someone would go to the trouble of breaking in for no discernible reason. This wasn't an intelligence deal. There was no vital information here—at least, none that he knew of. But there were some pretty valuable pawnables, which had been left untouched.

Lily edged closer, as if seeking reassurance. Absently he draped his arm over her shoulder. "Maybe somebody spooked him before he could start carting stuff out. There's a lot of traffic today."

"Is that what you think happened?" She wrapped her arm around his waist. Her head fit nicely in the hollow of his shoulder, and he tried not to think of the subtle wildflower fragrance, currently blended with sun, salt and barbecue sauce. "Curt, shouldn't we call somebody? What kind of law do they have here? Police? Sheriff's department? Park rangers?"

His brain busy running through the possibilities, he didn't bother to answer until she caught a fistful of shirt. "Listen, Curt, I know about this kind of thing. I've had experience."

"Right. You had some pervert making harassing calls and bringing you gifts."

She pulled away, making him thoroughly ashamed of himself.

"Sorry, that wasn't fair. Lily, sooner or later the cops

will catch up with your phone stalker.'' It would be later, if at all, but he didn't think she needed to hear that.

"Just give me just five minutes alone with him," she muttered ominously. "He'll never dial another phone, I can promise you that."

He hugged her to his side again. "Think you're pretty tough, don't you? Honey, leave it to the cops, they know what to look for. There's a lot of really bad stuff on the streets these days. Too many people strung out on drugs. Don't even think of going after this guy by yourself, leave it to the professionals."

She took a deep breath, started to say something, then stopped. He tipped her face up and said, "Lily? Are you okay? You feeling shaky or something?"

Another deep breath. Then, without looking at him, she said, "My mother was—that is, I was a crack baby. Do you know what that means?"

If she'd slugged him in the gut, she couldn't have done any more damage. "A—you were a what?"

"You heard me. My mother was an addict. She tried— she told me she tried real hard once she knew she was pregnant, but her friends—she had lots of friends—they didn't want her off the stuff. They—she—well, they all did drugs and…and other stuff. Before I was born, I mean. And after…" She was staring a hole in the window screen, as if the broad, placid vista outside could overcome the ugly memories.

Curt was holding her, rocking her in his arms, and she went on talking, her words muffled against his chest. "They couldn't do as much in those days about—you know—the way we were when we were born. Those of us who lived were—we had… But I'm tough. I was born tough, and I learned how to take care of myself." The utter conviction in her voice nearly finished him off.

Drugs for arms. Arms for drugs. It was a vicious circle, one he'd been battling, along with other special ops, for years.

Now he knew why. "Ah, Lily, Lily—yeah, you're tough." He wanted to hold her and protect her from every rotten thing that had ever happened to her. Retroactively. How the devil had she managed to get from there to where she was now? A writer of something called romantic suspense.

Romance? And flowers on the table? And pale pearls around a delicate throat, and lace table covers and women lined up to buy her books and hear her voice—that soft, husky, half-shy voice that came as such a surprise?

He was beginning to understand a few of the contradictions that were Lily. The stubborn in-your-face attitude that was so much at odds with the woman he'd first met signing books for a bunch of adoring fans. The woman who put flowers on his front porch. The glimpses of wariness he'd noticed, the childlike wonder and delight over a doe and fawn. All the contradictions that were Lily.

"Shh, stop shaking," he said, rocking her in his arms as if she were that infant who had come into the world so tragically abused, so fragile. "Annie, don't—"

Annie? Where the devil had that come from?

She lifted her head and stared up at him, her eyes shadowed, but dry. "You called me Annie. Is Annie someone special? There was an Annie in Bess's diaries."

"I don't even know an Annie. No Anne, no Annabelle, no Annette." Slowly he shook his head. "I know a Lily, though, and she strikes me as a woman who could do with supper, a drink, a hot bath and bed, in that order."

"We need to report it."

"To report what? That we think someone was inside

our house, but nothing was stolen, nothing was disturbed, no sign of forced entry?''

"You haven't even looked to see if there's any sign of forced entry. The back door was open. He could have come in that way.''

"The hell it was,'' he said softly. Setting her aside, he wheeled toward the door.

Lily grabbed a fistful of his shirt and matched her stride to his. "You're not going out there alone.''

"I thought you were into ducking for cover. I'll be right back as soon as I check out the padlock.''

"Check it all you want, but I'm going with you in case you need back up.''

He turned to glare her into silence, but then he shook his head, a reluctant smile creasing his lean, weathered face. "Lily, would you let go of my shirt?'' By that time they were in the pantry off the kitchen that led out onto the small back stoop.

"We should've brought your gun.''

He started to tell her the last thing he needed was a baby-sitter, then changed his mind. Silently they moved through the small pantry, past empty wooden bins that had once stored flour and meal and beans, past shelves that were empty except for a basket of wooden clothespins and a stack of paper sacks.

The back door hung open. One look was all it took to see that the new padlock had been cut through with bolt cutters. Curt started swearing, but broke off when Lily wedged herself up against his side.

"I didn't even notice,'' she said, "I'm so used to seeing it open.''

There was still more than an hour of daylight left, but the shadows were already deepening. Curt scanned the area for footprints. For lug soles in a men's size 9 1/2.

"I probably messed up any evidence," Lily said rue-fully. "I wanted to get the clothes off the line so we could make sandwiches."

"Yeah, well—the sand's too soft around the porch to hold a clear print, anyway."

"Know what I hate most? Having a stranger break into your home, even if he doesn't actually steal anything. It's a rotten, miserable feeling, as if you've been violated."

He was beginning to understand on a personal level—a gut level—what he'd understood only intellectually before. No wonder she'd been so spooked she had agreed to go off with a perfect stranger rather than stay in a place where some creep could come and go at will.

And now this.

Lily waited for him to go back inside. She had no in-tention of letting him out of her sight anytime soon. Not until whoever was moving in and out of his house was hauled off to jail. The fact that nothing had been stolen either this time or the last didn't make her feel any safer—just the opposite, if anything. Stuff could be replaced. She kept her back up disks in her tote, and that never left her side. But she could remember a time not too many years ago when about all she'd had to lose had been her Reeboks and her virginity.

At least she'd managed to hang on to one of the two.

Curt took one last look at the neatly cut padlock. "No point in hoping for fingerprints," he said. "Anyone who came armed with bolt cutters would know enough to wear gloves."

Lily nodded knowingly. Most of the street punks she'd spent her early life avoiding were too dumb to wear gloves. Shoot, snatch and run was their modus operandi.

Suddenly he turned and strode back through the house,

not waiting for her to follow. She scrambled after him, yelling, "What is it? Curt! What's wrong now?"

Back in his bedroom, he was standing before the open closet when she caught up with him. "Tell me! What's wrong? Damn your macho, tough-guy pride, *tell* me!"

"My boots."

"Your boots," she repeated. She waited, trying to picture him wearing a pair of heavy waders. Moving closer, she stared at the clutter of shoes, metal tanks, tubes and various unidentifiable black neoprene shapes. By contrast, her own apartment was neat as a pin. "Are you sure they're not there?"

He sighed. And then he hunkered down in a way that had to be ruinous on legs that had been shot at and sliced open and Lord knows what else. She touched his shoulder to regain his attention. "Were they special boots? Um— diving boots?"

"Yeah, they were special. Custom-made, with eel-skin panels and a starfish and trident design. Not another pair like 'em in the world. Damn things cost me a month's pay, and I never even got to wear 'em."

He sounded so—so plaintive, Lily didn't know whether to laugh or commiserate. *Eel-skin boots with starfish and tridents?*

The mind boggled.

"Go ahead and laugh. I don't blame you. Obviously, you never lost something important."

Only my childhood, she was tempted to say, but didn't because she had already said more than she'd ever intended to say. More than he wanted to hear.

"I lost a...a pair of shoes once. I guess that's sort of the same thing. Relatively speaking, that is. I bought 'em with my first paycheck from the cleaning service I worked for."

He tried to stand, settled back, but made it on the second try. "They were probably pretty miserable, anyway. I don't have Western-styled feet."

"One good thing—it shouldn't be too hard to spot someone who's hobbling around in eel-skin boots decorated with starfish and whatchamacallits, right?"

That got another of his rare grins, and Lily tried to think of something else cheerful, or at least hopeful, to say. "Why don't I make sandwiches while you call the cops?"

What she'd much rather do—not that she would—was to wrap him in her arms and hold on to him for the foreseeable future. Lust was bad enough. She could deal with lust because she knew where it led, which was precisely nowhere. But lust mixed with tenderness?

No way.

He followed her out into the hall. Paused, as if there was something he wanted to say, then shook his head and turned toward the phone. Lily waited until he punched in the number, wondering if it wouldn't be best if she left first thing tomorrow. Or even tonight. It was getting out of hand, this feeling of wanting to say something, do something—anything—to get him to react.

Which didn't even make sense, she told herself as she headed for the kitchen to construct the kind of sandwich a man would need to keep up his strength. Her kitchen skills were about on a par with his, but between them they managed to satisfy their appetites.

At least, their appetite for food...

He joined her just as she was pouring drinks. "Is anyone coming out?"

"Deputy sheriff's on the way, but there was a big pileup just north of Buxton. It's probably going to be a couple of hours before he can get up here."

"Then we might as well go ahead and eat."

By mutual consent they headed for the front porch. Across the highway, across the tops of the dunes, Curt could see the ocean. The distant horizon. It had a calming effect, and right now he could do with a dose of tranquility. It wasn't the break-in. As a crime, that was little more than a minor irritation, relatively speaking. Even with the loss of his boots. He was used to dealing with crime on a far larger scale.

It was Lily. What she had said about being a crack baby. All the term implied.

But it was far more than that, it was the woman herself.

Out of a clear, blue sky, as if she'd tuned in to his thoughts, she said, "You know something? I've been mugged. Twice I was nearly raped. I used to get beaten up before I got smart enough to disappear at the first sign of trouble. I've been robbed more times than I can remember—not that I had much to steal. I think the worst was when I was thirteen and someone stole a whole box of Krispy Kreme doughnuts I'd bought for my birthday."

Curt couldn't have spoken if his life depended on it. Carefully, he sat his beer on the railing, his sandwich on the fish box. He waited for what came next, a feeling of cold dread in the pit of his belly.

She took a big bite of her sandwich, a thoughtful look on her face as she chewed and swallowed. Then she reached for her tea, and he wanted to shake her, to grab her, to yell at her.

"What I mean is that you don't have to worry about me falling apart on you. I'm cool under pressure. Way cool. You might have gotten the impression—back in Norfolk, I mean—that I was freaked out, and I have to admit that a few years of soft living didn't do my reflexes any good. You probably thought I was scared, but actually what I was, was mad as the devil. But I get over mad real quick, and even if I'd stayed there, I could've handled it just fine. So this—'' she waved her sandwich expressively ''—this is no big deal. We report it, replace the padlocks, maybe get a dog or something—I always wanted a dog, but my apartment has this rule.''

"Lily, listen to me—"

But she was on a roll. "I'm sorry about your boots, but the last thing you need is something that hurts your feet. I mean, you have enough troubles as it is.''

"Lily, dammit!''

"Well, anyway, about a dog? In one of my books this woman got herself a rottweiler, and the villain fed him a poisoned pork chop, but the dog had been trained not to take food from strangers, and then in *Blood Relations,* I had this old woman with a houseful of yappy little mongrels, and nobody could even step inside the front gate without setting them off. So if I were you, I'd think about—''

Curt stood, reached down and removed the glass from her hand. He placed her half-eaten sandwich beside his own. And then he hauled her up into his arms and shut her up, using an unorthodox, if highly effective method. Efficiency, after all, was second nature to a man with his years of training.

He kissed her. Told himself all that talking had to be the leading edge of hysteria—told himself she needed calming, reassuring—told himself everything but the truth, and the truth was that even watching her eat turned him on like a battery of klieg lights.

His timing couldn't have been worse, but this thing had been building for days. Now, with the heightened tension—with the revelations about her past, about who she was and just how far she had come—the situation had reached critical mass.

And she felt it, too. She clung to him like moss to an oak tree. As if she'd been born to cling to him, her hands touching every part of him within reach. She clutched at his shoulders, raking her nails down his back, sending the kind of signals to his engorged groin that were the last thing he needed at this point.

Drawing back to catch her breath, she gasped, "Curt, please—could we—"

"Not a good idea, Lily." Giving lie to the words, his hands went right on stroking her breasts through her bra, under her loose shirt, even as the feel of her nipples, hard against his palms drove him ever closer to the edge.

"But couldn't we just—"

"Let's not complicate things," he made himself say. Famous last words of the seasoned warrior, the officer and gentleman.

"I won't complicate anything, I promise." Her hands flattened against his chest, slid down his rib cage to his belt, and he sucked in his breath. If she touched him there, he wouldn't be responsible for his actions. Gentleman or not, he might take her right here on the front porch, in front of a steady stream of post-Labor-Day traffic.

His brain continued to issue orders that his body continued to ignore. Capturing her hand, he pressed it against his diaphragm—then moved it lower. *Way to go, man. Why not just fall on your sword and be done with it?* Her fingers closed around him and he groaned.

Lily gasped. She was shivering like a halyard in a gale-force wind. Her breathing was harsh and irregular, but then, his own was no better. "Lily, Lily—honey, you're upset. Let's think this thing through first."

"Let's not. I don't feel like thinking anymore."

"Then I'll think for both of us. It's a tough job, but somebody has to do it."

He thought she chuckled, but he couldn't be sure. Think? It was all he could do to remain vertical. Obeying an instinct older than man, he widened his stance and lifted her so that his bulge nudged her cleft. Resting his chin on her hair—on the place where those unexpected cowlicks never failed to slip under his guard—he breathed in the clean, wildflower scent of her hair, her skin. Desire escalated into compulsion, compulsion to obsession. He wanted closer, wanted inside her, even as the last whisper of sanity whispered that sex might no longer be enough.

Ah, Lily, Lily, don't do this to me.

But she was doing it, all right, and he was letting her. Enabling, it was called. What was it about this particular woman? He'd known prettier women. Smarter women. The only trouble was, they weren't Lily.

"What's wrong?" Her lips moved against the sensitized skin on his neck. "Are you still mad at me for buying your family papers at the auction?"

"Am I what?" Clear symptom of oxygen-starvation. All the blood was pooled below his belt.

"Curt, if I hadn't bought the lot, somebody else would've, or else they'd have ended up in the city landfill."

"It's not—Lily, we need to—" He couldn't even manage to piece together a coherent sentence.

"I know I'm not the most beautiful woman in the world, but I'm no Halloween spook, either. So why don't you kiss me again and take me to bed, and then we can deal with the deputy without all this—this sexual tension messing things up."

He couldn't believe he was hearing what he was hearing. "Lily, listen—"

"No, you listen to me, Curt Powers, you've been parading around in front of me all week in those skintight trunks, and leaving your razor right next to my toothbrush, and—and—well, I'm only human, you know.''

If she'd leveled a twelve-gauge shotgun at him, he couldn't have been any more stunned. He dropped his arms and backed away. "Is that what you want? Sex? Because that's all it would be, Lily. No strings, no demands, no regrets.''

He could see her throat move as she swallowed, but she nodded gamely. "Well, I know that, for heaven's sake. You don't think I want to spend the rest of my life with a sorehead like you, in a place like this, do you? I just thought as long as we're here—consenting adults, and all that, I mean—and well, why not? It's not as if we're indifferent to each other. That is, I'm not.''

Lily waited for God to strike her dead. It wasn't the first time she'd done something foolish. She had never claimed to be the brightest woman in the world. It was, however, the first time she'd done something irreversibly stupid. And this was. If she went through with it—if he did it, that is, if they did it together—then she would never again be the same woman.

But then, that was the point, wasn't it? No more wondering what all the whoop-de-do was all about? All the stuff she wrote in her books, that she'd never even come close to experiencing? Faking it was all very well, but if sex truly was the most earth-shattering, mind-bending thing that could happen to a woman—with the right man—then why deprive herself of a beautiful experience? She wasn't getting any younger.

It was unfortunate that Curt Powers turned out to be the right man, but there you were—these things just happened sometimes. She wasn't like her mother. She wasn't doing it for money or drugs or anything ugly. Not that she was going to pin any romantic tags on it, because no matter what she might feel…for him it was only chemistry. That stuff bugs exuded. Phero-something-or-other.

And once she did it, she could tuck the experience away in her bag of tricks and write about it again and again, and maybe bring out the memory now and then to comfort her in what was probably going to be a solitary old age. Because she had definitely met the right man, only he wasn't available. Not long-term, and certainly not to her.

"So…will you?" If it sounded as if she was talking through clenched teeth, it was because she was. Her jaw was practically locked with embarrassment and because she was afraid that either he was going to refuse or she was going to pull her usual stunt and run away.

Curt studied her long and hard, taking in the stubborn set of her jaw, the uncertain, almost pleading look in her eyes. Oh, yeah, his brain was definitely starved of oxygen, the reasons embarrassingly obvious. There was no way in hell he could hide the condition he was in when she was practically begging for what he'd been wanting almost from the first time he'd laid eyes on her. Certainly the second.

Even so, he felt compelled to remind her that the deputy sheriff was on his way. To give her—to give them both— one last chance to come to their senses.

"But not right away. There was that accident, remember?"

What he remembered was all the reasons why he should just toss her baggage in her car, slap her on the rear bumper and send her off with whatever papers she wanted. Hell, she could have the lot. He would like to believe he still had enough integrity not to take advantage of a woman who was a little off in the head. A woman who thought she'd been sent here on some kind of mission to immortalize his batty great-great-aunt.

But she was making it damned hard.

Lily stepped closer. Tensing, Curt stood his ground. She reached up and brushed her lips against his. Her hands slid inside his shirt and found his nipples. Nail hard, they telegraphed a message where no message was needed. It was called sensory overload.

"Lily, think about it—I don't want to—"

"I do. Please, Curt? I've never felt like this before."

If she'd been some by-the-hour bimbo, he wouldn't have wasted time talking, but this was Lily.

Lilith. Female demon rumored to hang out in desolate places.

Oh, yeah, he'd heard all about Lilith. If this was her twenty-first-century incarnation, then he was in way over his head.

Nine

Halfway to the bedroom, Curt swept her up in his arms. "Last chance," he warned, wondering what he'd do if she took him up on the escape clause.

Instead, she tugged his face down to hers and rubbed her parted lips against his mouth. "You're supposed to kiss me back," she murmured.

It was all he could do to carry her. If he had to kiss her, too, they'd both end up sprawled on the floor. He told himself there were ninety-nine reasons to walk away and not one damned reason to follow through. Somebody's bluff had just been called, and for the life of him, he wasn't sure which one of them was the caller and which the callee.

His lower back protested with a warning twinge. Valiantly he ignored it. He made it as far as the bed, dropped the woman on top of the heap of line-dried laundry she had dumped there. Just as he collapsed beside her, she rolled her onto her back and lifted her arms in a sweet gesture of welcome.

There were winners and losers in any game, and this was the oldest game in the world. Curt told himself that he didn't want Lily to end up on the losing side, but at this point the alternative wasn't too appealing, either.

"You're thinking," she whispered, searching his face for...something she wasn't going to find there. "You think too much."

So he quit thinking and covered her mouth with a hungry kiss.

His subconscious mind took over as his conscious mind shut down. It was called situation awareness. Skin like richest cream. Just beneath the silken surface, a strength, a resilience he was only now coming to appreciate. The heady scent of arousal, mixed with what he'd come to think of as Essence of Lily. "Lily—are you sure?"

His advance warning systems—the clanging bells, the prickly awareness—were out of commission. There was only the muffled roar of surf and the more intimate sound of quick, harsh breathing. Curt told himself that if he had to stop now, he could do it, but it might be days before he could walk in an upright position.

"Too many clothes," she complained. "I want to see you."

If it weren't for the flimsy barrier of clothing between them, he thought with desperate amusement, he would be rearing over her like a maddened stallion. He reached for the buttons of her shirt. Fingers that could disarm a bomb so sensitive that a harsh word would set it off were defeated by a simple buttonhole. He gave up and ripped. Buttons flew, striking the floor like a handful of rice thrown at a wedding.

Bad analogy.

Encouraged by his frustration, which she obviously took for eagerness, Lily attacked his belt buckle. "Careful, there," he whispered hoarsely.

They managed between them to shed enough clothes so the rest didn't matter. Her bra was around her waist. It could wait. The world could wait.

Lily couldn't. "Don't be so blasted gentle," she growled. "Don't treat me like a lady, treat me like a woman!" Impatient, desperately afraid even now that he wasn't going to take what she offered—equally afraid he would—she tugged at his shirt, managed to pull it over his head and fling it across the room.

It was going to happen. Lily had made up her mind. But it had to happen now, before she lost her nerve. "Oh, my, you're…"

A bitter bark of laughter nearly sent her scurrying for cover, but she'd gone too far now to retreat. The earthy scent of him, the contrasting textures of smooth, tanned skin and crisp, wiry hair—muscles that leaped at the touch of her hands—

Too much. The old Lily would be cowering in a closet by now, but the new Lily—the woman Curt Powers had created—that Lily knew what she wanted. She refused to be denied.

First one and then the other took the lead, demanding access, staking a claim to each new discovery. The foothills of her small breasts—the valley between them. The shallow canyons where his muscular thighs swelled from the crease of his groin. Her fingers brushed against the crisp thicket of pelvic hair and the ridged plain of his abdomen…and then slipped lower.

Restraining her hand, he kissed her again, in a way that was totally carnal, a prelude to the act it foreshadowed.

Then, lifting his head, he gulped in a shuddering gasp of air and stared down at her. Slowly he shook his head.

Taking it for rejection, Lily pleaded, "Please—please, Curt, don't stop now."

She was embarrassingly wet between her legs. And while technically she knew what to expect, never in her wildest dreams could she have imagined the sheer force of all these tumultuous feelings.

Well, perhaps in her dreams.

Last chance. All ashore that's going ashore. Another broken, meaningless phrase raced through her mind. *Man the lifeboats!*

"Curt, you don't have to do this," she managed to say. "Maybe we'd better talk about it first." Those blasted diaries. Here she was drowning, and she was waving off her last chance of rescue.

"Changed your mind? It's not too late." His voice was so strained it was barely audible.

It was too late. It had been too late the first time she'd ever laid eyes on him, pinning her with those laser eyes of his, moving toward her like a great, stalking, tawny-haired cat. Unable to help herself, Lily lowered her gaze to his fully aroused sex, shut her eyes and said quickly, "I haven't changed my mind. Just…just do it, will you?"

Eyes still closed, she waited. And waited some more. With her heart pounding like a kettledrum, he could've shouted in her ear and she might not have heard him. At least he didn't attack her. He didn't get up, walk out and slam the door. And he didn't laugh. So she opened her eyes and peered up at him.

He was staring back at her. Unable to meet his gaze, she stared at his chest—at the dark-brown nipples, circled with hair, that were standing erect like small nail heads.

"Lily, what the hell is going on here? I think you'd better level with me before this goes any further."

Last chance. She could have escaped with a few shreds of dignity intact. Instead, she was lying there like a willing victim, waiting for him to make up his mind whether or not she was worth the effort.

Dammit, she was no victim. That was the whole point of this entire exercise, she told herself, needing desperately to believe it. For years she'd been promising herself that when the time came, she would be the one to choose instead of having the choice ripped from her by force.

Well, the time had come and she had chosen. This was the man, and if her timing wasn't perfect, then that was too bad, because it was probably the only chance she was going to get.

"Lily? Is there something you'd like to tell me?"

"Um. Well." *Way to go, lady.* "If you'd read any of my books, you'd know that I'm not at all shy about—you know. Sex. So we've been here together for a while, and you're—well, let's face it, you're not exactly dog food."

He made a choking sound. Lily forced herself to go on. This was hardly the scene she'd created in her mind titled The Deflowering of Lily. She should have been wearing something seductive. Candlelight had always figured somewhere in her love scenes. Instead, here she was, strip, stark naked except for the bra around her waist, with this particular man, out of all the men in the world. And all he was offering was sex. Nothing more. Not a single sweet, seductive whisper.

Actually, he hadn't even offered, she'd had to beg.

"Well, anyway," she said, and did her best to look sexy and sophisticated and experienced and very, very cool about the whole scene, when cool was the last thing she felt. "Anyway, I thought, why not? I mean, I've thought about it, and you have, too, because men can't hide that kind of thing,''

"Is that a fact?"

"Don't laugh at me. Don't you dare laugh! If you're not interested, just say so. Or maybe you're just not up to it yet. I know you're still recovering from whatever happened to you, so if you want to opt out, feel free. My feelings won't be hurt, I assure you."

She reminded herself that she was the one in control here. While he might be physically stronger, she was onto him now. She knew his weakness. He was an honorable man, and honorable men were no match for a woman who knew every sneaky trick in the book. She could take him easy, if it came to that.

Not even to herself did she attempt to define *taking him*. All she knew was that she had never wanted anything so much in her entire life as she wanted this man. Parts of her body she usually took for granted were throbbing with every beat of her heart. Lately she'd been dreaming dreams she didn't even know *how* to dream.

"Well," she said gruffly, "are we going to talk it to death, or are we going to do it?" She glared up at him, wishing she could think of an appropriate line. Something like, "I want to have your baby." The trouble was, writing about it and actually doing it were far different things.

Carefully he rose up on his knees, bringing his torso into clear view. She had touched him almost everywhere but there. His naked sex. She'd wanted to, had even dared to try, but he'd caught her hand, and she'd thought maybe that was something he didn't like. It wasn't the first time she'd seen an unclothed male body. Unfortunately, she'd seen more than she'd ever wanted to. She used to have nightmares about them, but that was then and this was now.

And this was Curt.

She told herself she probably didn't love him. She wasn't sure what love even felt like. She was sure of only one thing—that if this wasn't love, then it was as close as she was ever likely to get to the real thing. Whatever it was, it was the only reason she was here in his bed. A clear case of now or never, she thought sadly.

He was beautiful, scars and all. More rangy than brawny. His features weren't perfect—taken alone, they weren't even close. Odd that he should turn out to be the one man out of all the men she'd ever met, all the men she had ever written about. The one.

And his sex—

Oh, my. She stared—couldn't help herself, even knowing he was watching. "Well, you looked at me," she said defensively, and he nodded.

So she took her time, looked her fill, telling herself that even though it looked impossible, it was going to work. She knew all about everything—in theory, at least. She knew that nature took over at the proper time, doing whatever was necessary to make Part A fit comfortably into Part B.

Curt allowed her to stare at him. Bold as brass, he told himself, no longer quite believing it, even though she'd been the one to proposition him instead of the other way around. He wasn't going to rush her. If she wanted to do the driving, the least a gentleman could do was oblige her, even if it killed him. Which it damned well might.

He waited, the outside world fading away as the intoxicating scent of sex drifted up around him like some exotic, mind-altering spice.

Lily's thighs kept shifting, parting. She kept forgetting to breathe and having to gulp air like a drowning woman. Crazy, incredible feelings invaded the most intimate parts of her body, but she was in charge, she really, truly was, because this whole thing had been her idea.

Bending slowly—carefully—he took her nipple in his mouth and suckled gently, and then not so gently. And then he moved lower. She gasped, knowing what was coming next because she'd read books on technique and, after all, she'd written countless love scenes.

But mere words lost all meaning when it was actually happening.

"Oh, oh, oh…!" Helpless against the renewed surge of passion, she lifted her hips, silently begging him for release—for relief.

When it came, it was shattering. He rose over her, a tight, strained look on his face. She was ready. Wildly, breathlessly ready. Frantically she grasped at his shoulders, slippery with sweat, urging him on.

The last thing Curt needed was urging. Sex hadn't been a part of the prescribed recovery program. It had been a long time for him, but she was a desirable woman. She was available. Hell, she'd started this business—the least he could do was oblige her. If sex with a Navy SEAL came under the heading of research, then he was willing to do his part for the sake of literature—do it if it killed him.

Which it well might.

Years of the most rigorous training rose to the occasion. He forced himself to take his time instead of doing what he wanted to do, which was jump her bones and ride her until they both collapsed. Her timing was less than optimum, but he was determined to make this a memorable experience. Good sex was all he could offer—all he intended to offer—and even good sex might be beyond him in his present condition. He had a feeling that in spite of the way she'd exploded before, she wasn't quite as experienced as she wanted him to believe.

Gently, he moved his hand over her warm, damp thicket, preparing her for his entrance. She stared up at him, her eyes nearly black with arousal. Like one of those carnivorous plants, her legs came together, trapping his hand. She was ready. He told himself he was a fool to hold back. *Get in, get the job done, get out,* he thought grimly.

But this was Lily. She deserved the best he could offer—patience, at the very least. Except for that first time, when they'd both been fully clothed, he hadn't dared let her touch him, knowing what would happen. Premature detonation. He'd been primed far too long as it was. Now, taking her hand, he moved it down his body, closing her fingers around him…and then he sucked in his breath and snatched her hand away.

"I'm sorry," she said plaintively.

"No, honey, don't—it's… The thing is, it's been a long time for me, and I'm running a short, fast-burning fuse." Plus, his back was already issuing a few warnings of its own.

"Then why don't we just do it?"

A bark of laughter escaped. "*Do it?* Like…now?"

She nodded. He tried to come up with something suave, such as "Your wish is my command," but by that time words were out of the question. Ignoring the ominous tightening muscles in his lower back, he spread her legs farther, positioned himself and stroked her, using first his thumb and then the head of his member.

She was primed and ready. He was long past ready. And so he thrust into her.

She bucked wildly. He thought she might have cried out, but he couldn't be sure, he was too busy swearing. He couldn't stop thrusting, even when he knew—he *knew!*

Too late. He was drowning, and there wasn't one damned thing he could do about it but ride it out.

Moments later, utterly spent, he collapsed on her, sweating like a horse, feeling lower than dirt—feeling that indescribable sensation that came from mind-altering sex. The trouble was, this time it was mixed up with guilt and anger and confusion.

Anger won out. "So what was I, honey—a guinea pig?"

When time passed and she didn't speak, he rolled off, grimacing as spasms of another kind began in earnest. "You want to tell me what this was all about, Lily? You were a virgin. A damned virgin!"

"Well, it's hardly against the law." There was a red area on her neck where his beard had chafed her skin. God knows what other damage he'd managed to inflict. Aside from the obvious. He didn't even want to think about the fact that he'd just had unprotected sex with a stranger.

"Where the hell were your brains? If you're going to proposition a strange man, at least be sure you're carrying protection!" He waited. No response. He could hear her breathing, which was the only indication that he hadn't killed her. He knew he'd hurt her, but he refused to accept the entire blame for that.

"I don't have anything, um—communicable. I've been tested."

She'd been tested. Which meant that regardless of what she'd led him to believe, she'd obviously engaged in some type of risky behavior at some point in her life.

"Drugs?" he ventured, but he knew better. Not with her history. She wouldn't even touch a beer.

His back wasn't going to let up anytime soon, not without help. The deputy would be pulling up any minute now. There was no time to go into it, so he said, "We're going to have to talk, Lily. Only, right now, we'd better get dressed before we have company.''

She started to speak, broke off, then tried again. "All right, if it'll make you feel any better…" It wouldn't, but he let that pass. "I'm sorry. And yes, I deliberately used you because—well, because it was time, and I wanted it to be my choice. Me in charge, you know?''

He gave it all the consideration he thought it warranted. "Okay, so you were in charge. Did I perform to suit you? Any complaints? You want to critique my technique? You want to show me what I did wrong so next time I can get it right?'' He was seething with anger, and at this point, he didn't care who knew it.

"I…well, I don't know. I mean, it's supposed to be pretty great, isn't it? The books say that even the first time, it might hurt, but the hurt goes away and then there's this terrific, earth-shattering explosion of pleasure—pulsating rainbows and all that.'' She broke off, sounding confused, sounding embarrassed, making him feel guilty in spite of the fact that he was mad as hell.

"Yeah, I guess that about sums it up. I wouldn't use those words, exactly, but…close enough, I guess. Didn't happen, huh? Not for you?''

"Maybe if we tried again? It's not supposed to hurt after the first time, so maybe if we try it again, I'll get the full effect.''

He had to laugh. It nearly killed him, lying stiff as an oak six-by-six, afraid to do any more damage to his back than he'd already accomplished. "I think what's called for is a hot bath. Maybe with some salt thrown in. You—that is, you're bound to be sore, so maybe it would be best if we postponed the second act.''

"Oh. I guess I shouldn't have asked.''

Curt closed his eyes and prayed for delivery. From what,

he couldn't have said. From the naked woman in his bed who was all but begging for round two? Or the back that was killing him with each breath he took? "Look, I'm just thinking of you—of how sore you're going to be if you don't take precautions. I can deal with the sheriff."

Precautions. Oh, man, that was another problem. He set it aside to handle when he had more time. At the moment he needed to get rid of her so that he could roll off the bed and crawl as far as the footlocker where he kept the high-powered stuff he'd quit taking nearly a month ago.

Watching her try to cover her bare backside with a shirt—his, not hers—he thought about how he'd come down here to finish recovering, to simplify his life in order to figure out what he wanted to do with the rest of it.

Oh, yeah, he'd simplified, all right. "Way to go, Powers."

With a groan he couldn't quite suppress, he closed his eyes, clenched his jaw and rolled off the bed onto his knees. One problem at a time was about all he could handle.

Problem number one was Lily.

Ten

Lily heard him in the kitchen. He was making no effort to be quiet, slamming cabinet doors, scraping chairs. She knew when he ran water, because the water she was running in the stained, claw-footed tub slowed to a trickle.

She had heard the lid of his footlocker slam down, and because she knew that was where he kept his medicines, she allowed guilt to flow over her, along with the hot, weak-tea-colored water.

She'd forgotten to add salt. Just as well. While salt might help heal her more-obvious injury, the deepest hurt was hidden away inside her heart. That, she would have to deal with later—or live with for the rest of her life.

As for the other—sex, even with the right man, had been one big, flaming disappointment. All promise, but a little short on delivery. A lot short on delivery. Oh, the promise had been glorious beyond belief, but she'd desperately needed more. The ending had been all wrong.

Sighing, she slapped the wet washcloth over her breast and told herself to grow up and stop thinking like a romance writer. She'd had a few bells and whistles. If she'd expected the full marching band—expected him to suddenly realize he loved her—then she might as well start breathing again. It wasn't going to happen. She had done her very best not to put pressure on him—emotional pressure, that was. Because whatever love was, she was pretty sure it couldn't be coerced.

She knew for a fact that it couldn't be bartered, because her mother had gone that route. It was a dead end. Literally.

As near as Lily could figure out—and she was supposed to be something of an expert on the subject—love was something that happened spontaneously. Like snow. Like rainbows. Like, you open your eyes one day and whammo! There it is.

"Correct me if I'm wrong, Bess, but can love give you a sick feeling sometimes? Like running until your tongue's hanging out to catch the bus for the most important appointment of your life and watching it drive off without you?"

She should've settled for friendship. They'd been getting along so well—he'd even told her about his family, the ones that had come after Bess and old Matthew. Not much, because he didn't know much more about his family than she did about hers, but at least he knew who his were. He'd never been close to his mother, at least not since she had taken him away from his father and then lied and told him his father was dead. Lily had never been close to her own mother, because her mother had been lost long before Lily ever came on the scene.

"Something else we have in common," she murmured, pulling the plug at the foot of the tub.

But Curt at least could remember his father. Remember the stories he'd told, anyway. Lily didn't even know her father's name. Worse, she was pretty sure her mother hadn't known. She remembered asking once, after she'd learned that some kids had one father who lived with them all the time and hardly ever even hit them.

Her mother had looked at her and started crying, and then whatsisface had come in and started yelling at her, and Lily had crept away to hide in her favorite hiding place with the sticky all-day sucker and a book she'd stolen from the library.

"Lily! Wake up in there, we've got company."

Company. Oh, Lord, the sheriff. Curt's cowboy boots.

"Coming!" He probably needed to get in here, she thought, feeling guilty for trying to soak away this mess she'd got herself in. It was almost as if Bess had been egging her on, whispering "Go for it, girl!" Or the nineteenth-century equivalent.

Lily was coming to know the woman almost too well. She knew, for instance, that after remaining a spinster for most of her life, Bess had married herself a husband. One Horace Bagby, Esquire. That last she intended to look up as soon as she got back to Norfolk, but she thought it meant he was a lawyer.

"Lily?"

"I said I'm coming!"

Draped in a bath towel for lack of anything better, she hurried to her room and scrambled into the first thing she could lay hands on. Her hair was a tangled mess, and there were red patches on the side of her neck and one cheek, not to mention her breasts.

When she emerged from the house, the three men were standing out beside Curt's truck, the two uniformed deputies looking barely old enough to shave. Curt was wearing the khakis he'd been wearing before she'd practically torn them off his body, along with a faded denim shirt. All three men stood as if they were saluting the flag. Stiff, solemn.

Curt waved her over, and she forced a smile, then thought better of it. They'd been robbed, after all. This was serious business. Only trouble was, she couldn't seem to keep her mind on his lost cowboy boots when she had her own losses to deal with. *Deep breath. Think of it as research. Weird things a writer might someday need to know.*

Such as the fact that deputy sheriffs didn't sweat. Even with the sun down, the temperature was still in the high eighties. Not a bead of sweat in sight. Creases down the backs of their shirts and the front of their pants so sharp they had to have been preordained.

Curt made the introductions. One of the men murmured acknowledgment, and the other one nodded solemnly.

"Anything you want to add?" Curt asked her. He'd obviously taken a pain pill. She could usually tell, because the twin creases between his eyebrows weren't quite as pronounced.

"You told them about the boots? And the first time? The other night?"

He nodded. She tried to ignore the speculation in the eyes of the two young men, but it was clear what they were thinking. Does she or doesn't she? Has she or hasn't she?

She had. Although judging from Curt's expressionless face, he'd already forgotten about it. Maybe the whole episode had been only one of her wilder flights of fancy. Except there was the soreness between her legs and a growing misery that felt sort of like the flu, only worse.

One of the lawmen slapped a mosquito. The other one jotted down something on a small pad, then tore off the page and handed it to Curt. Seeing that they were about to leave, Lily turned away, resisting the urge to invite them in for a sandwich and a glass of iced tea. Anything to postpone the inevitable confrontation.

The old house looked more desolate than ever in 'her present frame of mind. The least he could do was to plant a damned flower or something! "It's not that he doesn't care, Bess, he simply doesn't know any better. His mama never taught him to appreciate the finer things of life."

She waited on the front porch, swatting mosquitoes, waving them out of her face, watching the man standing in the driveway. She'd never seen any man who looked so alone. She felt like crying, but instead she lifted her eyes and stared at the sky. Jupiter was rising, followed by tiny, distant Saturn. She knew because she had looked it up in a book on planets and constellations in an effort to learn how the wishing star myth had started. That had been for her second book, the one where she'd killed off nearly half a village and then made the chief of police fall in love with the prime suspect.

She knew better now than to wish. Once upon a time she'd had a silver-plated spoon with the silver mostly worn off. She remembered sleeping with it, feeling safe as long as she could rub her thumb in the smooth bowl. *Make a wish, Lily. Make a wish on the spoon, and it'll come true.*

It never had, of course. She'd known better, even then, but she'd desperately needed something to cling to, and a magic spoon had seemed better than nothing.

"You okay?" Curt had waited until the two men had driven off before heading back to the house.

"Sure," she replied, shrugging as if to prove it. Then she spoiled the effect by shivering.

"Ah, honey, don't do that."

"I'm not doing anything," she snapped.

He opened his arms, and she was tempted. More tempted than he would ever know. Fortunately, she had better sense. "I'm just hungry," she snarled, ready to pick a fight. Anything was better than throwing herself at him and howling her heart out.

His skeptical look said he wasn't buying it, but he let her get away with it, all the same. "I guess we never got around to finishing supper, did we?"

"No, I don't believe we ever did," she replied with saccharine sweetness. She could toss everything in her car and leave, or wait until tomorrow so that she could spend a little more time wallowing in humiliation, rejection and all those other rotten, nonproductive emotions.

It was a no-brainer. She would do what she had always done, which was to stand tall, pretend like crazy and then go home and rewrite the script, giving herself a better part. Maybe she should've been an actress instead of a writer.

"I'll make more sandwiches." Lily, in the role of gracious hostess.

"Fine. I'll pry loose enough ice cubes for your tea."

"By the way, I'm thinking of leaving tomorrow," she said airily a few minutes later. After working side by side in silence, tossing together a makeshift meal, they had adjourned to the living room.

Curt nodded and sipped his beer. He'd had three today. Two past his limit, especially when he was back on pain pills.

She was leaving. It wasn't as if he hadn't known it. Hell, he'd counted on it—it was the only reason he'd let her come here. He'd told himself he could handle anything for a limited time. He'd proved it too often for there to be any doubt in his mind.

"So...if you're sure you don't want Bess's novels, I

might as well take them off your hands," she said with a careless air that wasn't at all convincing.

"Sure. What about the diaries. You want those, too?"

"I'll take whatever you don't want." She took one bite of her sandwich and laid it aside.

The trouble was he no longer knew what he wanted. He'd come to the island because he'd needed a place to hole up, recuperate and make up his mind whether to get out of the Navy and look for another line of work, or stay in and hold down a desk. He was in line for a promotion. His diving days might be over, but he still had a lot to offer.

But somewhere along the line, things had changed. The parameters had shifted. Lily had happened. At this point he could lay it all on the table, the good and bad, including what had happened the last time he'd asked a woman to marry him—and try to make sense of what was happening now.

Not that there was any comparison. He hadn't even gotten that far with Lily. As for Alicia, he could no longer remember what the big attraction had been. He only knew that when he'd found out she was keeping score—that he was the fifth SEAL scalp she'd nailed to her bedpost—he'd walked out. Dropped the diamond he'd been about to give her in the kitchen sink and switched on the disposal. A real class act all around.

He cleared his throat. "Lily, listen, we need to—"

When the phone rang at his side, he thought, *Saved by the bell.* A moment later he handed it to her. "It's for you."

Lily hesitated. He could see the fear in her eyes. "No one knows where I am but Davonda and Doris—my agent and my housekeeper."

"It was a woman," he said, and watched the relief come flooding back to her eyes.

"Hello? Doris? What's wrong, has something happened?"

Curt listened unabashedly to the one-sided conversation, watching her expressive face. How could eyes so clear hide so many secrets? He could have sworn she was on the level, but then, he'd believed Alicia, too. From the first time he'd laid eyes on Lily, all dolled up like an admiral's wife, she'd been pitching him curves. She used words he'd never even heard, and then tripped over terms that were common coinage. She wore pearls and sneakers with holes in the toes. She seemed perfectly content in an unpainted ruin in the middle of nowhere, with a refrigerator that held only two ice trays, yet according to the biography in the back of her books she lived in seclusion in a swank area in Virginia and traveled frequently abroad.

The apartment he'd seen was adequate—even pleasant. Swank, it was not.

What if everything she had told him about herself was a lie? The crack-baby story—all of it?

He heard her say, "I'm so sorry—yes, I know, but—well, yes, of course. These things happen. Doris, are you sure you're all right? Because you sound like something's worrying you. Is it your feet? My plants?"

Light from the overhead fixture shone down on her hair, giving it a look of polished mahogany. He could see his marks on her skin, and wished he'd taken the time to shave first. Next time he would.

Next time, hell, there wouldn't be a next time.

"Problems?" he inquired when she handed him the phone. She was frowning.

"I'm not sure," she said thoughtfully. "I've lost my housekeeper."

"Hire another one."

"Doris and I were—that is, I thought we were friends."

"Even friends can retire."

"I never thought of her as old enough to retire. She has a son who lives at home—from a few things she's said, I think he's probably old enough to get a job and move out, but he won't, so she really needs to work."

"Maybe she just doesn't like working for a celebrity."

She gave him a look that was pure Lily. He'd come to expect them—even to provoke them. "You think I'm some kind of prima donna? Ha! Doris has never even read one of my books. I've given her autographed copies of every one I've ever written, even the paperbacks. She says she doesn't have time to read, but I happen to know she reads every word of the *Star* and the *Enquirer.*"

Their eyes met in shared amusement—one of those odd moments of intimacy that had nothing to do with sex. Curt heard himself saying, "I'm going to miss you."

She studied the frayed toe of one sneaker, seemingly unaffected, but he was on to her now. So he pushed his luck. "Why not hang around a few more days? I've got a guy coming next week to fence in the cemetery and straighten the tombstones. If that's really Bess out there, I'm pretty sure she'd appreciate your, um…"

"It's Bess. At least, I'm pretty sure that's her name on the stone—and the one that's fallen over is probably Horace. I wonder what he was like. Bess never said in her diaries."

"Well, there you go—we'll prop up Horace's monument, police the grounds and have us a rededication, or whatever it's called. I'll even order flowers for the occasion."

She appeared to be considering it. Curt couldn't believe he was going to such lengths to keep her around, when only a couple of weeks ago she'd been number one on his hit list—the woman who'd stolen his legacy. Less than an hour ago she'd made him forget the lessons of a lifetime.

"Do you know a Jackson Powers?"

"A what?"

"It's a who. I think he might be a distant cousin or something. I came across a postcard from Virginia Beach from this guy named Jackson Powers? It was addressed to your father—that is, to M. C. Powers here at Powers Point."

There might have been a time when the discovery of a long-lost relative would have meant something to him, but at the moment he had more important things on his mind. Such as how to keep Lily here until they could resolve this thing between them. He was pretty sure she couldn't be pregnant, not after only one shot, but all the same...

"Hang on a minute, I'll go get it. I used it as a place mark in the diary I'm reading." Headed for the door, she was moving like a saddle-sore dude after her first trail ride.

He made a mental note to buy one of those test kits from the drugstore. Maybe two or three, in case the first one screwed up. It wasn't going to happen, but still...another Powers at Powers Point? How many generations would that make?

He was starting to smile when he heard her scream.

On his feet before he had time to think, he was already halfway down the hall when he thought of grabbing his gun. No time. He'd have to rely on the element of surprise, if he hadn't already blown it. Flattened against the wall, he edged to a position that would give him the clearest advantage. He was flexing his fingers, his mind racing through possible scenarios. If the guy had a gun on her, there might be one split second when his attention would be diverted. He would just have to make it count.

No gun, no guy—nothing. She was alone. Standing in the middle of the floor, staring at her canvas tote, a look of utter horror on her face. "It—Curt, my bag moved. It *moved!* I saw it!"

The air went clean out of his balloon. He looked first at Lily, then at the canvas satchel hanging on the back of the chair, then back at Lily again. "You're imagining things. Maybe if you'd turn on a light—"

"There! It did it again!"

"Lily, you're hallucinating. All this business with Bess—the break-in—you're a little overwrought, that's all." He didn't mention the other possible source of stress.

"I am not overwrought!" As if to prove it, she snatched the bag with two fingers, shuddered, turned it upside down and then flung it aside. "You see? There's my clutch purse, my cheese crackers, a Moon Pie, my pen and… Oh, God," she whispered.

The mouse looked around, sniffed the air, then scampered under the bed.

Curt couldn't help it, he howled.

"Don't laugh. Don't you dare laugh!" Lily whapped him on the chest with the side of her fist, and Curt caught her and held her against him before she could do any more damage. An angry Lily was not without resources.

"I hate rats! I've always hated rats, I'll hate rats until the day I die!"

He didn't bother to remind her of the way she'd calmly informed him that he had mice. No big deal, oh, no. No big deal at all.

He made a conscious effort not to laugh again; made another conscious effort to ignore the feel of her, all soft, warm flesh and delicate bones, pressed against his body. Predictably, heat began to pool in his lower regions. Talk about timing. To think he'd once been a highly trained, tightly disciplined fighting machine. Any discipline he'd ever possessed was long gone, shot to blazes. And the worst of it was that he couldn't even bring himself to regret it. Good thing his days as a team leader were over.

"So what about it? Want to hang around a few more days? Help me exterminate a few mice and fix up the cemetery?" He couldn't believe he was actually begging her to stay.

Yes, he could. That was the trouble—it was entirely too believable.

"I'm not spending another night in this room until that mouse is out of here," she vowed.

"Hey, we've got options. We'll shut Mickey up in your room, and you can share mine." Before she could come to her senses—or he could—he closed the door and led her along the hall to his bedroom. Cross ventilation be damned, he could plug in the electric fan for one night. "See, I don't keep food in my bedroom, so there's nothing to attract mice. We've already checked out my closet—no unauthorized personnel there, right? So first thing in the morning I'll get us some traps and lay in a supply of cheese."

"Peanuts."

"Peanuts?"

"They like peanuts even better than cheese." She was glued to his side, her usual independence nowhere in evidence. It wouldn't last, but at the moment it suited his purposes just fine.

"I could offer to sleep on the couch, but I don't have one."

She nodded. They both knew where this was leading. Since he'd taken her to bed that afternoon, he hadn't been able to think about anything else. It had been all he could do not to tell those two deputies to buzz off, that whatever was going on, he could handle it.

"Lily? You okay with this?" If she wanted out, then he'd have to let her go. He was counting on Bess to help him keep her here, though—at least until he worked up his courage to take the next step. At this point he wasn't even sure what it was, but he had his suspicions. Oh, yeah, he had those.

"Lily?"

"All right," she snapped.

"Want a shower before you turn in?"

"I had one. It's your turn."

"We could share—that is, if you're afraid to stay here alone?"

That drew a tiny smile, one of her gutsy, independent ones. "Me? Afraid? In your dreams."

In his dreams. That about said it all.

While Curt hastily smoothed the covers on his bed, Lily thought of all the things she'd read, and even written, about love scenes set in bathtubs, hot tubs and whirlpool baths. Somehow, an ancient claw-footed tub with iron stains and chipped porcelain seemed somewhat lacking as a setting for romance.

But then, in their case it wasn't romance, it was sex.

And she was going to do it, and enjoy every moment of it, because it would be her last chance. What's more, she wasn't going to cry when it was all over and she said goodbye. She would eat dirt before she let him see her shed a single tear.

"Oh, what the heck," she said with a small lift of her shoulders. "I might as well have another shower. I've got squashed mosquitoes all over me."

He didn't say a word, just gave her a shot from those high-voltage eyes of his that melted her bones, not to mention whatever common sense she possessed. She glared at him. "What!"

"Quit trying so damned hard to be tough. For now— just for tonight, be who you are."

That nearly finished her off. Her face crumbled, but she got her emotions under control and said coolly, "I don't know what you're talking about. Are we going to do it, or are we going to talk it to death?"

Curt lifted his eyes to the ceiling and thought, Of all the women in the world, why did it have to be this one? The one specifically designed to drive him up the nearest wall? "You know what your trouble is, O'Malley? You're afraid to admit you're a real woman. You've bought into your own publicity."

"I am not. I know exactly who I am."

He wanted to tell her—to make her believe—that the Lily he knew, the Lily who had shared his bed once before and was going to share it again, was real and wonderful and unique. That she made him a little crazy—a lot crazy—but that she'd added a dimension to his life he'd never even known existed.

"You've got one clean shirt left," she challenged. "Can I have it?"

"I owe you," he said solemnly. "I ripped the buttons off yours, remember?"

"How good are you with needle and thread?"

"Better than you are, I expect."

"That good, hmm?"

Hooking an arm around her shoulders, he led her down the hall to the bathroom. No curtains on the window, not even a shade. The shower curtain was the plain plastic variety. A less-romantic setting for what he had in mind would be hard to imagine, but he'd been afraid to leave her alone—afraid he might come back and discover she'd jammed the door shut, or worse, packed up and left. And he really did need a shower. All in all, it had been one hell of a day.

"Let me," he said when she started to remove her shirt. Replacing her hands with his, he eased the plain cotton garment over her shoulders, marveling all over again at how anyone so fragile could be so strong. How anyone so strong could be so vulnerable.

In no time at all, their clothes were scattered on the bathroom floor. Curt stepped into the tub first, then swung her over the side. She told him he was going to ruin his back, and he laughed and said, "Let me worry about my back."

"This is a really bad idea, you know? I thought it would be so—well, I mean, it always works in the books, but in real life, I'm not so sure we won't end up breaking something."

"Too late for second thoughts. Turn around, lift your face."

Lily didn't want to turn around. She didn't want to lift her face, but with Curt's hands on her shoulders, she seemed to have no will of her own. Tears filled her eyes and overflowed. She tried to pretend it was the shower, but they both knew the trickle of water wasn't responsible. "Don't look at me," she grumbled. "Soap in my eyes— I'll be fine in just a minute."

Curt looked. What he saw brought home a truth he was nowhere near ready to accept. "Quit squirming," he growled, and plastered a handful of lather on her chest.

Somehow, they got through the process without coming to grief. It helped that the tub had been thoroughly scoured by sand. Helped even more that the water had long since run cold, which tended to discourage a man's ardor. Marginally.

He was determined to make it last—to make up for what had happened before. This time was for Lily. And if there was no next time...

Well, he would just have to deal with it.

"Feel my goose bumps?" Lily laughed shakily as he slowly worked a palmful of lather down her side. Then his hand moved between her thighs, and she gasped and went still.

"Are you still sore here?" Cold water or not, one touch and he was so hard he ached, but if it killed him, he refused to hurt her again. There were other ways...

Lily closed her eyes. Her head fell back, her hair dark with moisture, her lashes fanning out on her high cheekbones. Instead of a direct reply, she reached out and touched him. "Are you?" she asked, all innocence.

He nearly went up in flames. At the feel of her touch—hesitant, then bolder—his whole body stiffened. He could have sworn his mind blacked out for an instant. Indescribable sensations flooded through him, an urgent desire that was fully as powerful as release.

Capturing her hand, he eased it away before he shamed himself. A man thirty-six years old should have more control. Control had never been a problem before—at least not since he was about sixteen.

But then, he'd never made love to Lily before.

"Come on, let's get out of here," he growled. Feeling behind him, he wrenched off the flow of water, then lifted her out of the tub and somehow managed to climb out himself without collapsing.

Lily blotted his face with a towel and then her own. Her red-rimmed eyes glowed with an incandescence that robbed him of what little breath he had left. He touched the place on her throat where his beard had abraded her tender skin and said, "I forgot to shave first. It'll only take a minute."

"Don't you dare," she whispered fiercely. Catching his hand, she tugged him down the hall to his room, the night air cool on their damp bodies. If she was still worried about mice she didn't mention it.

The last thing he remembered thinking as they fell into bed together was that he had little to offer her but himself. It might not be enough for a woman whose career made her a celebrity, when his own career could take him away at a moment's notice, often for months at a time.

Eleven

They made love slowly, carefully, tenderly the first time. Lily saw all the rainbows, heard the bells and whistles, felt the earth move. All this she told him, proudly, shyly, when she could speak again. She was beaming—couldn't seem to stop smiling.

Curt looked as if he wanted to cry, but was too much of a man to give in to tears. "I know lots of other ways," she confided. "I've written about—well, actually, I read about them first, but then when I started to write, it sort of came to me, the way things do. Your subconscious mind knows so much more than your conscious mind does—the trick is to pry it open."

Lying beside her, he smiled and traced the rim of her ear. "Anyone ever tell you you've got beautiful ears?"

"Mmm...no." Maybe he needed time to rest, she thought. He'd been injured—she still wasn't sure of all the details, but she knew his back hurt him when he exerted himself. They'd both exerted themselves, but it had been worth it. Oh, my, yes-s-s, she thought smugly.

"Wanna try out a few more possibilities?" His voice resonated in the oddest parts of her body. She wondered if that was a part of it—like the response of plumage in breeding birds.

"Are you sure you're up to it?"

"Try me," he suggested, and she did. With his willing cooperation. By the time the first pale hint of morning crept through the open window, Lily felt well and truly loved, even though not a word of love had been spoken.

She awoke early, watching the way the first shafts of morning light brought out the gold in his hair, along with the silver. His beard was showing again, even though he'd insisted on getting out of bed to shave after the first time they'd made love.

Or maybe the second. She was having trouble remembering. For a man who claimed to be considering retirement, he had more stamina than the law allowed. She owed him a backrub, and he owed her a cat. Sometime during the most glorious night of her life, they had come to those terms.

And if she'd hoped for something more than a cat, then it wouldn't be the first time she'd been disappointed.

"Hungry?" he murmured beside her.

"Aren't I always?"

"Yeah, but I'm talking food."

She laughed aloud. And that was another thing—he made her laugh. Somehow, she'd forgotten how, if she'd ever learned. And he laughed, too. From the grim, suspicious man who had first accosted her in the bookstore and accused her of stealing his property, he'd come a long way.

They both had.

* * *

Curt left soon after that for his early-morning workout on the beach. Lily felt tired, yet she was compelled to get up, to do something. She was bursting with energy. Was that a side effect of sex? Funny—she'd never read about that one.

She was on her knees with a knife and a spoon, the only gardening tools she could find—by the time the sun cleared away the morning haze. Whatever happened, she was determined to get this done. The idea had been growing ever since she'd first noticed the bright red and yellow flowers blooming all over the beach.

"This is for you, Bess, in case I don't make the rededication or whatever." She dug and planted and patted. Three on each side of the steps sounded about right.

"Where? More to the left?" She glanced over her shoulder and frowned. Curt was still at the beach. There was no one else around, but she could have sworn she heard someone saying...

Must be my imagination, she told herself. She was just patting the sand around the last of the plants when she spotted Curt jogging across the highway. Stiffly she rose to her feet and waved. "Come see what I've done," she called out.

"Yeah? What's this supposed to be?"

"Um—landscaping?"

Slowly he shook his head. "Where'd you get the plants?"

Puzzled, Lily gestured with her spoon. "Over there— across the highway. There's millions and millions of them, blooming out here in the middle of nowhere. I thought it would be nice if..." Uncertainly her voice tapered off.

"Lily, that happens to be a national park. It's Federal property."

"So? What's your point?"

He raked his fingers through his hair, sighed and said, "No point, I guess. Why don't I help you water them?"

Driving south toward Avon some hour and a half later, Curt told himself the last thing he needed was a house cat. Maybe he could just borrow one. Rent one?

It wasn't as if he'd be there permanently.

It all came down to Lily. He didn't know if she would want to stay at Powers Point—or go with him wherever he was sent—or if she'd even have him. Talk about putting the cart before the horse.

An hour later he was headed north again, with a box of Krispy Kreme doughnuts, half a dozen fish he was going to have to dress and cook, and a cat, compliments of his father's old friend, Charlie. "Easy there, partner, it won't be long now. You're going to pig out on mice once I turn you loose in the house." Or maybe on fish. It all depended on how good he was at cleaning the things and how eager Lily was to try her hand at cooking. Maybe he should have bought a cookbook while he was at it.

Burdened with a newspaper-wrapped bundle, a grocery sack and one large cardboard box, he called from the front door. No answer. He'd half expected to see her on the porch, her nose buried in one of Bess's diaries again.

"Hey, Lily, come see what I brought...."

In the open doorway he came to a dead stop, every cell in his body suddenly on full alert.

"I got your boots back," she said grimly, nodding toward the pair of eel-skin boots with the distinctive starfish and trident design lying on their sides on the floor. They were halfway down the hall, between her bedroom and the office. She was holding his 9 mm with both hands, arms braced, feet spread, dead-aimed at a poor son of a gun with a straggly beard, who looked ready to collapse.

"You wanna clue me in?" he asked mildly.

"It's him. I knew it before he even opened his mouth."

"Right, it's him," he repeated numbly. And then he caught sight of a scrap of purple lace. Slowly he looked back at the cowering wretch who was blubbering something about his mama. "Why, you sorry bastard. You aren't fit to—and you even stole my boots!" The jerk wore one earring. It was a clip-on.

"He's my stalker. He brought me a gift, see? Purple panties."

"I brought a...a flower, too, but it blew out the window."

"The window of what?" Curt eased up beside her and removed the gun from her hands without incident. The poor devil looked ready to crawl on his knees and beg, but Curt knew better than to take chances. He could be a walking chemical lab, which could make him dangerous at worst, unpredictable at best. "You want to call the dispatcher, Lily? Fill her in on what we've got and have her send Fred and Elmo back."

"Tie him up," Lily growled. "Tie him up with those awful things he brought me. One thing about nylon, it doesn't break easily."

She marched out, still keyed up from the encounter, then wheeled around and came back. Shaking her finger at the poor sot who looked as if he would like to crawl under the linoleum, she said, "I'm going to call your mother, too. No wonder she felt as though she had to quit. If I had a son like you, I'd resign from the human race!" To Curt she said, "He not only stole my phone number from Doris's purse, he had a duplicate key made—even after I'd changed the lock." Her cheeks were splotched with color, her fists clenched at her sides. "You...you—I can't even think of a word!"

So much for running away and hiding, Curt thought with reluctant admiration.

It was more than an hour before the two deputies drove off with their tearful prisoner. By then Curt was almost afraid to open the cat box. The fish were starting to smell ripe, and ants had discovered the doughnuts.

Gingerly he reached for the sturdy cardboard carton. He'd cut holes in the sides. A gray paw curled out of one hole, claws fully unsheathed. "Sorry, cat—something came up."

Lily crouched beside the box, making soft, cooing sounds in her throat. "Oh, I love gray cats."

"Yeah, well love this one from a distance. He's not in a particularly loving mood at the moment."

"We'll give him a fish."

"If he sticks around long enough. Stand back, here goes."

Roughly eight pounds of gray-furred fury leaped out of the box, made a run for the door, which Curt had taken care to shut. The animal turned to glare over its shoulder from a pair of malevolent green eyes, his ears flattened, his bushy tail twitching.

Lily said, "Oh, look at those eyes, aren't they gorgeous? Here, kitty, kitty, we won't hurt you."

"Don't even think about petting it yet."

"I'm pretty sure I read somewhere that cats can read minds. People minds, that is. And this one looks a lot smarter than your average cat, don't you think?"

"How many average cats have you ever known?" he asked.

"Well, none personally. That is, I've never had a pet, but there are always a few cats in any alley, on account of the garbage cans."

Awkwardly Curt managed to stand without too much

actual pain. "Obviously, this wasn't one of my better ideas."

"I think it was a great idea. That's right, honey, you keep your distance until you get us all figured out." She looked up at Curt, a smile on her face that came close to bringing him to his knees again. "Know what? I'm going to call her Bess. Don't you think that's perfect?"

Oh, yeah, perfect. "Honey, you can call him Eleanor Roosevelt if you want to. I don't think he'll mind at all."

The bad news was that Bess the tomcat probably wouldn't hang around any longer than it took him to punch out a screen.

The good news was that Lily would. If she was into planting stolen flowers and naming house pets, then that was good enough for him. Any loose ends—and there were going to be plenty of those—they could work out between them.

"How about next time we get us a female cat?" he suggested.

She stood and leaned against his side, beaming at their temporary tomcat. "Kittens. Now that would be nice, wouldn't it?"

"Oh, yeah, kittens would be just fine. Which reminds me, I stopped by the drugstore and picked up one of those test kits."

"Test kits. Am I supposed to know what you're talking about?"

"Pregnancy? Kids? Family? I figure if it doesn't turn the right color, we can keep on trying until it does, what do you say?"

Lily closed her eyes and whispered something under her breath. Curt felt pretty much the way he'd felt when he was buried up to his neck in mud, with a dozen or so arms dealers jabbing the jungle foliage with bayonets just inches away from his face.

"Well. If that's a proposal, then I say yes. If it's only a…a proposition, then I guess the answer's the same. Only I hope it isn't, because Bess and I have our standards."

Curt felt as if a dam inside him had broken. *Bess, whatever you are—wherever you are—I might need a little help here. My training didn't cover loving a woman who believes in ghosts, so hang around, will you?*

* * * * *

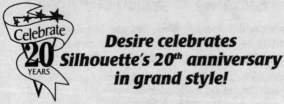

You're not going to believe this offer!

In October and November 2000, buy any two Harlequin or Silhouette books and save $10.00 off future purchases, or buy any three and save $20.00 off future purchases!

Just fill out this form and attach 2 proofs of purchase (cash register receipts) from October and November 2000 books and Harlequin will send you a coupon booklet worth a total savings of $10.00 off future purchases of Harlequin and Silhouette books in 2001. Send us 3 proofs of purchase and we will send you a coupon booklet worth a total savings of $20.00 off future purchases.

Saving money has never been this easy.

I accept your offer! Please send me a coupon booklet:

Name: _____

Address: _____ City: _____

State/Prov.: _____ Zip/Postal Code: _____

Optional Survey!

In a typical month, how many Harlequin or Silhouette books would you buy <u>new</u> at retail stores?

☐ Less than 1   ☐ 1   ☐ 2   ☐ 3 to 4   ☐ 5+

Which of the following statements best describes how you <u>buy</u> Harlequin or Silhouette books? Choose one answer only that <u>best</u> describes you.

☐ I am a regular buyer and reader
☐ I am a regular reader but buy only occasionally
☐ I only buy and read for specific times of the year, e.g. vacations
☐ I subscribe through Reader Service but also buy at retail stores
☐ I mainly borrow and buy only occasionally
☐ I am an occasional buyer and reader

Which of the following statements best describes how you <u>choose</u> the Harlequin and Silhouette series books you buy <u>new</u> at retail stores? By "series," we mean books within a particular line, such as *Harlequin PRESENTS* or *Silhouette SPECIAL EDITION*. Choose one answer only that <u>best</u> describes you.

☐ I only buy books from my favorite series
☐ I generally buy books from my favorite series but also buy books from other series on occasion
☐ I buy some books from my favorite series but also buy from many other series regularly
☐ I buy all types of books depending on my mood and what I find interesting and have no favorite series

Please send this form, along with your cash register receipts as proofs of purchase, to:
In the U.S.: Harlequin Books, P.O. Box 9057, Buffalo, NY 14269
In Canada: Harlequin Books, P.O. Box 622, Fort Erie, Ontario L2A 5X3
(Allow 4-6 weeks for delivery) Offer expires December 31, 2000.

PHQ4002

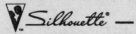

ATTENTION JOAN JOHNSTON FANS!

Silhouette Books is proud to present

HAWK'S WAY
BACHELORS

The first three novels in
the bestselling Hawk's Way series
now in one fabulous collection!

On Sale December 2000

THE RANCHER AND THE RUNAWAY BRIDE
Brawny rancher Adam Phillips has his hands full when
Tate Whitelaw's overprotective, bossy brothers show up with
shotguns in hand!

THE COWBOY AND THE PRINCESS
Ornery cowboy Faron Whitelaw is caught off-guard
when breathtakingly beautiful Belinda Prescott proves to be
more than a gold digger!

THE WRANGLER AND THE RICH GIRL
Sparks fly when Texas debutante Candy Baylor makes handsome
horse breeder Garth Whitelaw an offer he can't refuse!

**HAWK'S WAY: Where the Whitelaws of Texas
run free...till passion brands their hearts.**

"Joan Johnston does contemporary Westerns to perfection."
—Publishers Weekly

Available at your favorite retail outlet.

Desire.

**the popular miniseries by
bestselling author**

ANNE McALLISTER

continues with

A COWBOY'S GIFT
November 2000 (SD #1329)

Bronc buster Gus Holt had shied away
from weddings since he'd ducked out of
his own a decade ago. But when ex-fiancée
Mary McLean turned up in Montana—
pregnant, alone and lovelier than ever—Gus
suddenly hankered to leave behind the
bunkhouse for a marriage bed!

Look for more **Code of the West** titles
coming to Silhouette Desire in 2001.

Available at your favorite retail outlet.

Where love comes alive™